HAVE YOU EVER WONDERED HOW BOOKS ARE MADE?

UCLan Publishing is an award-winning independent publisher, specialising in Children's and Young Adult books. Based at The University of Central Lancashire, this Preston-based publisher teaches MA Publishing students how to become industry professionals using the content and resources from its business; students are included at every stage of the publishing process and credited for the work that they contribute.

The business doesn't just help publishing students though. UCLan Publishing has supported the employability and real-life work skills for the University's Illustration, Acting, Translation, Animation, Photography, Film & TV students and many more. This is the beauty of books and stories; they fuel many other creative industries! The MA Publishing students are able to get involved from day one with the business and they acquire a behind the scenes experience of what it is like to work for a such a reputable independent.

The MA course was awarded a Times Higher Award (2018) for Innovation in the Arts and the business, UCLan Publishing, was awarded Best Newcomer at the Independent Publishing Guild (2019) for the ethos of teaching publishing using a commercial publishing house. As the business continues to grow, so too does the student experience upon entering this dynamic Masters course.

www.uclanpublishing.com
www.uclanpublishing.com/courses/
uclanpublishing@uclan.ac.uk

ANNE CASSIDY

THE
DROWNING
DAY

ILLUSTRATED BY JAKE ALEXANDER

uclanpublishing

The Drowning Day is a uclanpublishing book

First published in Great Britain in 2021 by
uclanpublishing
University of Central Lancashire
Preston, PR1 2HE, UK

978-1-912979-75-2

1 3 5 7 9 10 8 6 4 2

Set in 11/17pt Kingfisher by Becky Chilcott.

A CIP catalogue record for this book is available from the British Library.

Printed and bound in Great Britain by Clays Ltd, Elcograf S.p.A.

For Connor,
who thought this was a good idea.

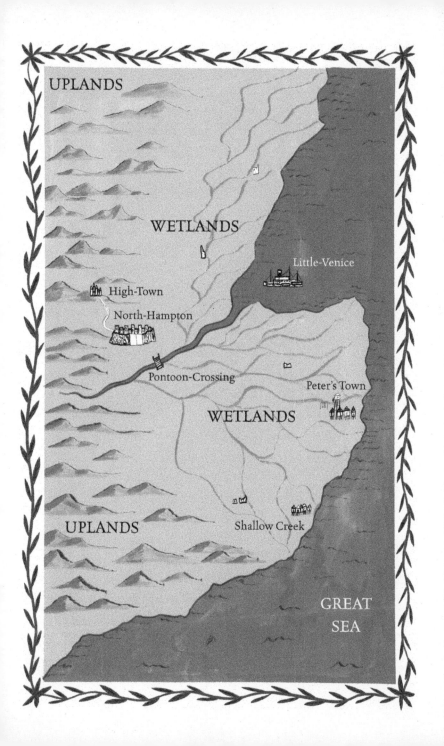

THE WETLANDS

ONE

THE WATER WAS COMING.

Jade stood on the jetty and looked far out to the sea. The surface was calm and the sky was dull. She couldn't see any signs of life. In the bay there were scores of boats, rafts and diving platforms, all tied to buoys. They clung together in groups, completely still. Like a past-world photograph. Further out were shoals of plastix bobbing on top of the water. They lay on the surface like a skin.

A breeze ruffled at her neck and she shivered a little. She took her timer out of her pocket and looked at it. Through the cracked glass she could see that it was thirteen hours. Time was moving too fast.

After weeks of rainfall, it was dry. The air was still and in the distance, through a grey haze, she could just make out a dull orange sun. She looked around the village, her eyes searching for any movement. Only the wild dogs walked through the mud, weaving in and out of the buildings. Many homes stood back from the sea, shored up by wooden struts forced deep into the ground. Above them all was the water tower, its steel legs dusted with rust. The village was here but the people had gone. The homers had taken everything that they could pack. She'd watched them depart yesterday and some that morning. Those who could pay went on the last bus, and then some families left in the backs of trucks and some on engine-bikes. The ponies dragged carts and the rest left on foot this morning, just as she would. The road out of the village had been saturated to start with, now it was cut up.

The siren sounded. It rang out across the Wetlands even though there was hardly anyone left to hear it. Jade headed back along the jetty and into the square. The sign for the evacuation was flapping on the news-board:

WARNING!
FLOODING IMMINENT!
ALL HOMERS SHOULD HEAD
FOR NORTH-HAMPTON!

Underneath was printed:

BY ORDER OF THE HIGH-WARDENS, JUNE 2052.

She headed towards home. Some of the dogs followed, wagging their tails, one or two barking and growling at each other. There was no food to spare so she had to ignore them.

Inside the porch was her back-sack, almost full. Her dollar-belt was already fastened around her waist. Her water-bag just needed topping up. She was ready to go anytime, but there was an ache in her chest.

She went further into the cabin, towards the main bedroom door. Pushing it gently, she saw the old man asleep in the bed. He looked pale. His arm was outside the covers, his hand thin and frail. He'd been like that for days now.

It would be a push to get to North-Hampton before they closed the gates, but she couldn't leave Peter's Town just yet.

She had to wait for her granddaddy to die.

TWO

DURING THE EVENING, WHEN HER GRANDDADDY WAS ASLEEP, Jade packed up bread and meat and some apples and walked to Bates's caravan. There was no sign of any of the dogs. Maybe they had given up and moved off somewhere else. This dismayed her. Without dogs, the rats would come.

Bates lived on the edge of the village. She found him sitting out in front of his caravan beside a small fire that he'd lit.

'How's Frank?' he said.

'Sleeping.'

'Is he in pain?'

'I don't think so. He's just tired all the time, exhausted.'

She held out a bag. It was a tarpaulin back-sack, one of a few that her granddaddy had made years before. Living in the Wetlands, it was important to keep belongings dry.

'Here, use this to take your stuff to North-Hampton. There's some food in there as well.'

'Thanks.'

Bates was twelve, the same age as her, but smaller and thinner, as if he hadn't always been able to get a good meal to eat. He looked scruffier than usual: his shirt was ripped at one sleeve and his jeans were threadbare at the knees. He had his peaked cap on so she couldn't quite see his eyes.

'And you'll go in the morning,' she said.

'Sure.'

The next day, Wednesday, was the last day of the sirens. The dykes at North-Hampton would close at sixteen hours on Thursday. Bates should have gone with the rest of the homers but he had wanted to wait for Jade. Up to now she'd been happy to let him, but time was moving on and the water was coming closer at every tide.

'You all packed up?' he said.

She nodded. She glanced over at the caravan he lived in. It had been damaged at one end, as if it had been in a collision. It was like lots of things in the village: old, from past-world, not fit for purpose anymore. Jade had often wondered if Bates had to build up the bottom end of his bed to stop himself sliding down in the night.

'Yes. What about you?'

'Won't take me five minutes.'

Bates didn't have much to pack. He had turned up one day, three months or so ago, in just the clothes he stood in. Some people from the village had helped him and found him somewhere to live.

'You could come and stay with us tonight. It's very dark and lonely here.'

'I'm used to it. Anyway, I think you and Frank should spend time together, seeing as . . .'

'I know.'

'What did Rosa say?' he said.

'Oh, you know. That it won't be long.'

Rosa, the village medic, had come round that lunchtime, just before the last trucks left. She had pulled Jade into the other room and spoken in a whisper.

Your granddaddy is going to die soon, Jade. I don't know how he's held on for so long. You'll want to avoid any discomfort for him so you should give him these pills. They'll help him on his way. It's a merciful thing to do.

She'd given Jade a small bag with pills in it.

Poppy-pills, she'd said. *Give him four to start off with. He'll be comfortable. He might go in his sleep. If not, give him the rest.*

Jade had clasped the bag and put it in her pocket.

'So, you need to go first thing,' Jade said to Bates, 'As soon as it's light. You promise me you'll go?'

'Sure,' Bates said, pulling the peak of his cap.

'It gives me less to worry about if I know you're gone.'

'I will. I promise.'

'Take care,' she said, 'and I'll see you in North-Hampton.'

THREE

SHE WALKED HOME.

The village was pitch black. There was only one pinprick of light and that was from the window of her own cabin. She stepped carefully, one dark shape merging with the next. The empty homes and silent pathways felt like somewhere strange and unknown.

She came to the children's play-park. The wind had strengthened and was pulling at her hair as she leaned on the trunk of the central tree. Cradle-swings had been looped over its sturdier branches and they swung around in the gusts. Day or night, there were always children in the play-park but now it was empty. Instead of hearing squeals and shouts, there was just the noise of the sea and the leaves brushing against each other. She thought about her sister, Mona, who she hadn't seen in nearly two years. Mona and the older kids often hung around the play-park in the evenings after the younger children had been called to bed. Granddaddy usually sent Jade along to fetch her home. *Tell that girl to get in here!* he'd say in a mock-angry voice, so Jade would hop along the pathways and find her sister leaning against the tree, whispering to friends or maybe talking to one of the boys.

Jade peeled a strip of bark off the trunk. She pulled it apart with her fingers and let it drop to the ground. Mona had been on her mind a lot in these last few weeks. After more than a year of not mentioning her name, Granddaddy had started talking about her. At first, Jade had been shocked but then she realised that the illness had taken all his anger away from him.

She stepped away from the tree trunk and caught one of the cradle-swings with her hand and straightened it. She sat on it and pushed at the ground with her foot, so that it moved gently back and forward.

His illness had taken a lot of things away from him. Up until then, everyone had known him as *Big Frank*. He was almost seventy but still working: diving every day, scavenging along the bay, hunting for past-world miscellanies. He'd done it ever since the Great Flood, often with his old diving partner, BB. People always said he was one of the best.

Together, they'd pulled anything and everything from the sea bed: machinery, wire contraptions, wheels, pistons, cogs; as well as more recognisable things like pots, pans, cutlery – even some past-world coins. All of it they sold; some to the ryders, some they took directly to North-Hampton. Anything from *before* had value. When BB travelled to other areas of the coast, her granddaddy had worked alone. He'd pulled out parts of at least six bi-cycles over the years, taken them to North-Hampton and come back with enough dollars to last for months.

The last few months, Big Frank hadn't been able to do much. Even picking up a glass of water had been a problem. His back was bent and his arms and legs were skinny. He had shrunk in height and the skin on his face looked one size too small for him, his big blue eyes poking out.

No one knew what was wrong. People who lived in the Wetlands usually got sickness because of insect bites or infections that couldn't be cured due to lack of medication. Or maybe they got bitten by a rat or fell from a roof or the water tower. But Big Frank had just got thinner. He was a shrinking man and he said it was because of the chemicals he'd swallowed under the water. Meds were no good, he said, even if they'd had the dollars to buy them.

The last week he'd been asleep a lot. When the sirens woke him up, he had talked about packing his maps, his diving gear, his valuables and heading for North-Hampton.

But he hadn't been able to get out of bed to do it. He'd laid back and began to talk about Mona and the dressing-up box that he'd got for her. He'd rambled a bit and repeated the same stories over again.

Rosa had said that he was delirious. *If you have to give him all the pills ,you should leave then. Don't wait for him to die.*

I'm not leaving him.

Jade had said it with conviction, but her heart was leaden. Rosa had left soon after.

Now she stood up off the cradle-swing. The wind ruffled it and she stepped back on to the path. She could hear the surf, the tide coming closer and closer every time. The earth beneath her feet was already starting to soften, to feel spongy.

She couldn't leave her granddaddy, not for one second.

FOUR

JADE PREPARED THE TABLETS. SHE SMASHED THEM UP WITH a fork and added honey. Her granddaddy was sleeping and she tried to wake him up. He stirred a little, opening his eyes. Jade spooned the mixture gently into his mouth. The old man raised his head for a moment and tried to grasp the silver key that hung on a chain around his neck. It seemed as if he was going to say something, but he just fell back asleep. The key flopped on to the bedclothes. Jade put her finger out and touched his arm.

He would sleep now and possibly not wake up. Sadness came over her and she walked away, afraid that she would cry again.

She picked up her back-sack and took it into her bedroom. On the windowsill were her books. She still had some room at the top of her bag, but the books would weigh it down too much so she had to leave them behind. Stories of adventure and mystery. Her granddaddy had bought most of them for her on their trips to North-Hampton. A couple were given to her by another homer, a girl called Kris, who had left the village some months before. She had spent hours with Kris; reading the stories, talking about the heroes, imagining that they were part of the adventure.

One of the books was different. Mona had given it to her. It was called *The Ballerina*, a past-world story about a girl who ran away from home to join a ballet troupe. Jade had thought it silly but Mona had loved it, and so Jade had read it with her sister now and then.

She lay down and listened to the sea. High tide had gone and now the water would slip away and the bay would be exposed – its muddy bed, the shells and rocks and stones that had settled there. Then, when the tide turned, the sea would start advancing again, coming back, claiming more of the land than it had before. At every new tide it would creep up the beach and then into the empty village.

She thought of Bates, alone in his caravan, surrounded by debris – bits of old machinery, tyres, broken furniture. At the edge of the village, he was prey to rats or other creatures. Even ferals had passed by. It wasn't a safe place.

Over the last few weeks, she'd asked him a number of times if he wanted to come at stay at their cabin but he'd always refused. He was a boy who found it hard to take kindness.

Most of the people in Peter's Town were poor. The places they lived in were little more than cabins, shacks or rusted trailers. The possessions they had were limited to what they could carry. It was the same for everyone who made a living by the side of the Great Sea. People fished, grew crops and kept livestock. They sold the fish at the pontoon-crossing market and they used the animals for milk and eggs. Or they scavenged, like Jade's granddaddy. The money that people got for their produce was used to feed themselves and keep warm in the winter.

Anyone from the age of twenty onwards went off to find work. If they actually had any money, they could buy their way in High-Town. Only the rich lived there.

Jade's mother had died when she was young and she had never known her father. It was like that for a lot of kids who lived in the Wetlands, the thirty or so villages along the coast. The men who had strength often joined one of the Militias or worked in the mines or on flood barriers. Many women and older boys went to North-Hampton and became domestics or were employed in small-industrials. Some Wetlanders ended up as ryders, biking everywhere in their orange bibs, buying and selling, transporting mail and miscellanies. People who left to find work rarely came back. Most of the groups who lived by Great Sea were the dreg ends of families. Groups of young and old people living together, some not even related. For a long time it had been Granddaddy, Mona and Jade. Then Mona left and it was just the two of them.

Bates had no one and didn't talk about his past.

She had been friendly to him, pulled him into what was left of her family. And he liked her granddaddy. She would find Bates on the bench at the jetty or sitting cross-legged in the garden while the old man was resting in a wicker chair. Big Frank told him stories about when he and BB used to dive for treasure in the bay.

She heard something from the next room. She got out of bed, picked up the oil lamp and went quietly into her granddaddy's room. She saw that he'd changed position. He'd turned over in his sleep and knocked the bowl from the side table on to the floor. She picked it up, the remnants of honey still at the bottom. It was the bowl where she'd mashed up the tablets that Rosa said would *help him on his way*.

She went back into her room and lingered at the windowsill. Then she picked up *The Ballerina*. She slid it into a pocket inside her back-sack.

FIVE

JADE WOKE JUST AFTER EIGHT HOURS. HER ROOM WAS FULL OF light and she struggled up, flustered at having slept so long. With a heavy heart she looked at the wall which separated her from her granddaddy. She listened, not expecting to hear anything, knowing that she had to go next door and find out if he had died in the night.

A feeling of dread took hold of her.

She tried to stay steady, pulling on her jeans and taking her time to lace up her boots. Pushing her hands into her shirt she heard an unexpected sound. There was *talking* outside the cabin. There were *voices* speaking. Astonished, she stepped out into the living room. The cabin door was wide open. She went across and stood behind it so that she could see better.

Outside, at the edge of the porch, she saw her granddaddy in the wicker chair. Bates was sitting opposite him on a stool.

Her mouth opened in surprise. He was *sitting up* and talking to Bates. His voice was clearer than it had been over the past days. She moved closer to the door so she could hear what they were saying. They were talking about the past.

'. . . you remember any stuff about the second flood?' Bates said.

There was a gap. Jade imagined her granddaddy thinking for a moment.

'I can never forget it. At the time, none of us could believe that anything bad was happening. The sea began to look fuller, faster in some way. Then one day, the tide came in higher than before and we looked at each other with disbelief.'

He stopped speaking, as if remembering the exact moment. Jade had heard this story many times.

'At every tide it seemed to come to a stop further up the beach. People in my village started to pack up but they weren't quick enough. "Lightning doesn't strike twice," they said but it did and within days the water was everywhere and we were fleeing, taking with us the things we could carry.'

Jade looked on with amazement. He hadn't had a proper conversation in weeks.

'I never believed it would happen again,' the old man said.

'And then it was over,' Bates said.

'We waited for weeks on high ground. Then we started to go back, hoping to find our homes, but the coast line had altered. Me, Mona and Jade, we camped every day and watched the water.'

He stopped to cough and Bates looked past him, straight at Jade. He caught her eye and gave the merest shake of his head in case she was going to interrupt.

'We didn't trust the sea. We thought of it as an enemy. Peter Johns, the oldest man in the village, stood on the headland and watched for days. Then he said it was all right so we started to build this village and we called it Peter's Town.'

Her granddaddy continued to cough. Jade walked out on to the porch and he looked round at her.

'Hey! Are you OK?'

'I'm good,' he gasped. 'I should be dead. But I'm not.'

'He's well, look!' Bates said.

Jade stepped across and put her hand on her granddaddy's shoulder. He was hot and she could feel the sharpness of his bones sticking through his nightshirt. His face seemed thinner again, his skin like paper, puckering around his mouth as he showed his teeth.

'I don't understand,' Jade said.

She thought of the poppy-pills she'd given him. Could it be that they had *cured* him? For a second, she pictured the rest of them, in the pouch, sitting in her back-sack.

'Good days and bad days,' Big Frank said, his voice raspy. 'I'm OK at the moment.'

'Not cured, though?'

'No, Jade,' he said, 'but OK for a while. Definitely enough time to get to North-Hampton.'

'There's medics there, they could help,' Bates said.

'Need to be miracle workers to help me.'

'But you could try . . .' he said.

'Let's get out of here, then. In case the water comes,' Big Frank said, coughing.

'But can you walk?' Jade said, knowing that he couldn't.

'Sure I can,' he said, breathing shallowly, a smile on his face. 'A little. But I won't need to. See what the boy brought.'

He pointed to the other side of the garden. She turned and looked. There, sitting on the grass next to the wash-house was a wheeling-chair. She couldn't quite believe it. She'd seen them in North-Hampton but never in the Wetlands.

'Where did that come from?'

'It was in the lock-up behind the Worship-Hall. I went looking this morning for anything to take to North-Hampton, bits of food and stuff, and I found this. Frank can sit on it. We can push him to the pontoon-crossing.'

She walked over to it. It was from past-world. It was covered in plastix and had big wheels each side. There was no engine attached though, so they'd have to push it.

'It's great, but it's more than thirty kilometres.'

'That's true . . . But it's worth a try . . .'

Jade couldn't speak. She should be happy. Her granddaddy was sitting up, speaking, lucid, *alive*. But all she could think of was how they would manage on a thirty-kilometre walk, pushing a very sick old man over the rough terrain between Peter's Town and North-Hampton. Would they get there before the gates of the dyke closed?

'The boy did well, Jade,' her granddaddy said, looking piercingly at her.

'He did, he did . . . Well done, Bates.'

She could give him more of the poppy tablets. They had revived him in some way. Maybe it would be possible to get as far as North-Hampton. It might even be possible to then take him to the Free-Clinic and see if he could be helped. It might be all right.

'We should pack your stuff,' she said, helping him to his feet, her hand under his arm as he walked unsteadily into the house.

'Good idea. I've not much to take.'

She left him sitting on his bed sorting through the drawer of his bedside table. She stepped outside the house so that she could think straight without having to pretend that everything was all right. Bates was squatting by the wheeling-chair feeling the tyres, looking at the spokes.

'You said you were leaving this morning, first thing,'

she said.

'I thought you'd be pleased with this.'

'I am. It's good but . . .'

'It'll be OK. You go and get Frank ready and we'll get on our way.'

She looked at the chair. The wheels were huge like those on a bi-cycle. It might be possible. It just might work. The sooner they got started the better.

SIX

JADE WAS PACKING. SHE PULLED OUT ONE OF HER GRANDDADDY'S shirts and stuffed it into her back-sack. He was half-sitting, half-lying on the bed, weaker all of a sudden, and she wondered if the poppy-pills had worn off. On the bedside table was a mug of hot tea sweetened with honey.

'Have you got my map, Jade? Must bring my map.'

His voice was cracked and he looked grey. There were shadows under his eyes.

Jade reached into a drawer and plucked out a leather pouch. Inside was a single map of past-world that had been cut into four quarters. It was old and faded, its corners curling. Jade had seen the pieces laid on the floor of the porch many times, although recently they'd stayed folded and hidden away.

'Let me see . . .'

She passed the pouch to him and he rifled inside it. Then she picked up the mug of tea and offered it to him but he waved it away. As she placed it back on the bedside table she felt her arm being gripped and heard indistinct words.

'What?' she said.

She moved closer to him.

'If I don't make it to North-Hampton . . . If I don't get that far, you have to do something for me.'

He closed his eyes and seemed to sink back into the pillow. She thought he might have slipped back into a sleep but his hand tightened on her arm.

'When you get to North-Hampton, go to Monks' Alley and find Charlie Diamond's shop. Monks' Alley – we used to go there, remember?'

She nodded. Her granddaddy coughed and fought for his breath.

'Charlie has something to give you. He will only give it to you if you have my key.'

He held out the key that hung round his neck.

'He will help you. He will be able to get you into High-Town.'

'That's enough talking . . .'

'You do remember Charlie's shop? In Monks' Alley?'

She nodded. She remembered the jeweller's shop in

North-Hampton. Granddaddy took his valuables there; things that were too special or rare to sell to the ryders. On those visits she and Mona had stayed outside. They'd looked at the precious items for sale in the window and Mona had pointed out what she would love to buy. Jade had mostly stared past the jewellery at the man in the shop, behind the counter. He was thin and stooped and had long white hair, parted in the middle. His name was *Diamond* and he sold jewels. That seemed funny to Jade and she'd told Mona about it but her sister had been too interested in what was in the window.

Her granddaddy had closed his eyes again. She went to move her arm away but he held on to it, speaking even though his eyes were shut.

'Spike came. A week, maybe two weeks ago. He brought me a package.'

She had to think for a minute. Spike? *The ryder?*

'Here.'

He pulled a tatty packet from his pouch. It was small but had been folded and folded, the corners square, the points in triangles. It was neat and had his name written on it. It made sense then. Spike was someone her granddaddy did business with. He had a bi-cycle which he'd painted a silver colour. He came by the village every now and again and took any valuables or letters up to North-Hampton. Granddaddy had been using him for years.

'Sit up,' she said.

She put her arm under the old man's back and pulled him up to a sitting position. She fed him some tea and he slumped on to the pillow, staring up at the ceiling.

'Open it, Jade . . .'

She picked up the brown paper package. She unfolded the corners like she'd done in the past when Spike or any of the other ryders brought packages. They may have contained dollars or razors or candies; sometimes clothes and sewing paraphernalia that Mona would use. There had even been books for her. This package was thin though and for a moment she wondered if it contained anything at all. When it was unfolded she saw a piece of card with a picture on it; an artist's drawing with colour. The words *Butterfly Palace* were above a sketch of a fancy building.

'What is this?' she said.

'It's where Mona is. Your sister is there, in High-Town. She's not well. She's not happy. I only heard when Spike came. I wanted to go to her but I couldn't . . .'

He stopped and caught his breath, as if he had been running.

'She needs me to help her – that's why I've got to get to North-Hampton. But if I don't make it, you must go to Charlie's and you must get into High-Town. Find your sister. Get her out of that place.'

Jade stared at the card with the picture of the building on

it. *Butterfly Palace*. It looked pretty – just the sort of place she thought that Mona might end up. It might be a minstrel-show house. She might be singing and dancing.

'It's a bad place, Jade. If I don't make it, you *have* to get her out.'

'I will, I will,' she said, stunned by the information.

'Charlie will give you something of mine. It has great value. Don't tell anyone,' he said, pulling himself up off the pillow. 'Don't tell *anyone* what he has given you. Don't trust anyone. Not even the boy . . .'

'Keep calm. It'll be all right,' she said.

His face was sharp with agitation. His jaw drawn back. His eyes pained.

'Let me go and get the chair. We'll get you to North-Hampton then you can talk to Charlie yourself. You rest. You rest, now.'

He nodded and lay back on the pillow. She stepped out of his room and took a moment to catch her breath.

Mona was in High-Town. She wasn't happy. She wasn't well.

Bates appeared at the door.

'Everything all right?' he said. 'We ought to get going.'

'Get the chair,' she said. 'Bring it inside. We can help granddaddy into it and then . . .'

Bates walked away to where the wheeling-chair was. She watched as he squatted down beside it and grunted as he pushed at a lever.

'The brake doesn't work so well, but we're not going up and down hills so it shouldn't matter.'

'OK...'

He pushed it over the grass, see-sawing over the uneven surface. She took one of the handles and helped him lift it across the porch stair. It fitted through the door and she moved the small kitchen table out of the way and tucked some chairs to the side so that it would wheel through towards the bedroom. All the time, she was thinking about Mona and how she had to get her granddaddy to North-Hampton so that he could find her. He was ill but maybe with poppy-pills they could revive him for a few days.

'Here's the chair,' she called out, manoeuvring it into his room.

He was lying in the same place, his head back on the pillow, his eyes closed.

'If we can get this alongside the bed, we can wake him up and lift him into it,' she said to Bates.

She glanced at the old man in the bed, laying still, his eyelids calm, his face rested.

'Wait...' she said.

She stepped across to the bed and bent down so that her face was level with his head.

'Granddaddy, you need to wake up now. We're going to get on our way.'

She put her hand on his shoulder and nudged it.

He didn't move.

'We should go,' she said, her voice louder.

A terrible feeling gripped her. She put out her finger and placed it her granddaddy's neck to feel for a pulse but there was no movement, no pumping motion, no beat, no sign of life.

Bates was behind her. She heard him sigh.

'He's gone,' she said.

She didn't know how to feel. She'd wanted it to happen. She'd prayed that it would happen so that she could leave. Her granddaddy had *wanted* to go. But now . . .

'Looks like we won't be needing the wheeling-chair after all,' Bates said.

SEVEN

THE FLAMES FROM THE PYRE LEAPT INTO THE SKY. BIG FRANK'S body lay on it. Jade and Bates had placed him there, along with some of his possessions. They'd covered him up with bedsheets and lit tiny piles of kindling around him.

The wheeling-chair sat alongside the Worship-Hall where it had come from.

Jade's fingers felt for the chain she had round her neck which held the key. It was tucked down her shirt. The pouch that held the old man's map and papers was in her back-sack. Her granddaddy's words were in her head.

Her heart was sore though. The line that had held her to the old man had snapped and he had floated away.

She thought of him diving, deep in the water, the surface further and further above him until he couldn't see the light anymore. She imagined him, in among the sea grass, unable to return. It cut a tiny crack across her heart. She heard the wood snapping as it burned. The wind pulled at her hair and she shivered a little. She thought about her sister, Mona, living in the Butterfly Palace, unwell and unhappy. She wouldn't know that her granddaddy had died.

Bates stoked the fire with a long stick.

She remembered Mona, years before, on the porch, sitting on the wicker chair with her feet up on the table. Her hair hung down the back. Her face was painted as usual, her lips as red as the cherries they sometimes brought home from the pontoon-market. *Honestly, will you look at that girl?* her granddaddy said, rolling his eyes. But he was proud of Mona and always smiled when she dressed up or performed songs and dances and plays for him. Jade would try the same thing; dancing, singing but it was never the same with her. *You're much more practical,* her granddaddy said, *you're someone I can depend on.*

'Should you say a prayer?' Bates said.

Jade shook her head.

'He didn't believe in any god.'

'You should say something though. It doesn't seem right to just . . .'

'I don't know what to say . . .' she said, blinking tears from her eyes, rubbing at her face with the back of her hand.

Bates looked agitated. Then he put his hands together as if in prayer and spoke.

'I liked Big Frank. I liked his stories about diving and I liked how friendly he was to me when I came to live here. His daughter will miss him and so will I. Amen.'

The pyre was engulfed with flame and she looked away, fearful for her granddaddy's body in such a blaze. Her eye settled on the memorial mounted on the wall of the Worship-Hall. It was a stone circle. She'd seen some others like it in North-Hampton.

IN REMEMBRANCE OF THE
GREAT FLOOD OF 2042
'THE DROWNING DAY'
AND THE SECOND FLOOD OF 2048.

WE WILL NEVER FORGET
THE MILLIONS WHO LOST
THEIR LIVES.

THE HIGH-WARDENS OF HIGH-TOWN

She looked back to the pyre. It seemed to have shrivelled in size, as if the old man had finally shrunk down to nothing. Bates edged her away.

'We should go,' he said. 'We don't know how far the next tide will come in.'

She couldn't move for a moment.

'Let's go. It's not yet midday. We might even get to the pontoon-crossing today.'

Jade picked up her stuff and let herself be led away from the pyre, feeling the flickers of heat on her back. They walked between the empty houses, past the play-park. She looked down into the bay. The sea was brown, slurping back and forth. It had covered the jetty. Soon it would spill into the houses around the bay. Her and her granddaddy's cabin would be one of the first to go.

As they left the last buildings, a rat ran past her foot and disappeared under one of the houses. It wouldn't be long before more of them came. It was their habitat, after all; soon it would belong to them again.

On the open path she stood for a moment and watched as the smoke trail from the pyre twisted up into the sky. Then she followed Bates into the Wetlands.

EIGHT

IT WAS A HARD WALK. THE PATHWAYS WERE MORE UNEVEN THAN Jade remembered. They'd been used by many trucks, bikes, carts and people and had been broken up. The engine-bikes had sprayed up stones and clumps of mud and the carts and footfall had worn the debris into place. She pushed herself, putting one foot after another, keen to get on.

They passed a lot of barren land; ditches, stretches of water, grasses, hidden rivulets. There were also abandoned homes, places left behind from past-world: old farms and outbuildings, a small industrial estate where water had rotted the foundations and allowed vegetation to grow up the sides. There were the shells of past-world mechanicals upside down where they'd been left by the second flood, their contents, their wheels, their metal fixings, picked apart by scavengers.

Bates tried to talk to her a few times but she didn't answer. 'It's all right,' he said, 'I know you're upset.'

She saw a siren-post. Silent now, it stood out boldly in the landscape; an ugly trunk of wood surrounded by thorn-wire. On the top was a wailing speaker that was given power by the sun.

A clump of trees and bushes gave some shade when they were ready for a break. Jade pulled out some bread and cheese from her pack. The cheese felt soft and rubbery and so did the bread, but she was hungry. She split it into two pieces.

When they started walking again it was baking hot, uncomfortable. In the distance, on another path, Jade could see some other homers making their way towards the pontoon-crossing. They were going slowly, two goats on tethers behind them. A number of ryders passed by in their orange bibs. Their engine-bikes were heavy with luggage or goods that people had paid them to take to North-Hampton. They sped past Jade and Bates and other homers, spraying up dirt and mud in their wake.

They didn't make the pontoon-crossing. It was an effort for her and Bates to get over ground that had been rutted and broken, some of it in mud, some stretches turning into small streams. There was plastix about, emerging from the impacted ground, much of it floating dully on the waterways. The path had crumbled away in places and fallen down into standing water.

At eighteen hours they stopped at a junction. The road ahead began to rise and it would have been difficult to carry on while they were tired. To the west was a path, an old farm track, and Jade could see some buildings. A curl of smoke rose from a fire that someone had set. There were people there, possibly stopping to break their journey to North-Hampton. The two of them had come twenty or more kilometres from the coast. The water wouldn't reach here yet, even if there was a sudden surge. It would be a good place to rest the night.

There were a dozen or so people in the yard. Every one of them stopped what they were doing and looked round at the two of them. Their faces were unfriendly, suspicious. The fire had been lit in the centre of a circle of stones that looked like it had been there for a long time. Resting across the top was an old tin pot with something bubbling in it.

Jade didn't recognise any of them. There were a couple of ryders dressed in leathers, with bi-cycles leaning up against walls. She gave a half-smile, trying to break up the tension but no one responded. They just stared. She could see Bates, out of the corner of her eye, looking worried. Was there going to be a row? She grabbed hold of her dollar-belt.

'What you looking at?' one of the men said.

'Nothing . . .' she said, stepping backwards.

Just then she heard someone call her name and she turned towards one of the outbuildings. Standing at a door was Rosa, the medic, who had left the village the day before.

'Jade! Did your granddaddy . . .'

'He passed this morning,' she called.

Rosa bustled towards her with her arms out. Around her neck hung the chunky red cross that she always wore when she was helping people. For a second, Jade felt embarrassed and didn't know what to do. She let Rosa hug her.

'I'm so sorry, sweetie,' she said. 'He was a lovely man.'

The medic stepped away and saw Bates. She patted him on the arm. Then she turned to the people around the fire.

'These are friends from my village. I will look after them,' she called out.

Jade walked after Rosa and could hear, from behind, the sound of murmurings from around the fire as conversations started up again.

'Pay no attention to them. Everyone's jumpy because there have been some ferals about. Come into this building. It's a bit broken down but at least it's got a roof. There's room for you to stay here tonight.'

Inside the door was a large space that looked like it had once been a kitchen; there was the bowl of a sink in the corner and remnants of wooden cupboards that had been attached to the wall. The windows had no glass and the floor was damp and spongy. In the corners, Jade could see vegetation growing upwards, green and slimy.

It was dim inside but cool.

Over in the corner were a group of people in a tight knot – a family, maybe. Rosa led them in the other direction towards someone sitting at an open door which was hanging off its hinges. Outside she could see a broken-down brick wall.

'Here's Mary. You remember her, Jade? She lived in our village for a while. Mary, here's Jade. She's just lost her granddaddy.'

Jade remembered her. People called her Old Mary. She travelled from village to village on foot. She slept in a tent and sold things that helped people's health: balms and cough mixtures. She used herbs and mysterious powders to make coctions which cured pains and fevers. She was ancient, much older than her granddaddy had been. Her face was thin and had many lines coming from her mouth and eyes, and her hair was white, hanging in a pigtail over one shoulder. She sprang up though and marched across to them like a young person. She put her hand out and shook Jade's hand powerfully.

'I'm sorry for your loss. It was Big Frank, the diver, wasn't it? I heard he had a sickness.'

She turned to Bates and shook his hand vigorously. Bates looked startled by the touch.

'I know you,' she said to Bates. 'You're William's boy. From Shallow Creek. I was there a year or so ago.'

'Shallow Creek?' Jade said.

Shallow Creek was along the coast from Peter's Town. Nobody went there much. Some people said that it was a place for robbers and thugs.

'You're mixing me up with someone else.'

'You might be right. William's boy was bigger maybe. Now, I'm not sure—'

Rosa interrupted, 'We can all rest in this part of the building. We'll have a fire outside the door and cook.'

'I thought you'd be in North-Hampton now. Why are you here?' Jade said.

'The truck we were on was overfull. Then we passed by a young man who couldn't walk. There was no room for him. So, we said we'd stay here tonight. The driver is Mary's grandson's friend and he says he'll come back tomorrow for us.'

'Let's get the fire going, shall we?' Old Mary said.

'How old is she?' Bates whispered, later, when Rosa was busy with the food.

'Some people say she's a hundred!' Jade said.

'She can't be.'

Jade shrugged. She found that she was smiling. Her granddaddy was finally at rest. There was hot food and a place to sleep and they were well over half way to North-Hampton, where she would get some information about her sister.

NINE

IT GOT DARK AS THEY SAT AROUND THE FIRE. AFTER THEY'D shared their food, Rosa and Old Mary started to sing quietly. The sound of it made Jade remember how Mona had sung all the time. Her granddaddy had taught Mona some old songs from when he was a young man and he was always asking her to sing them. People in the village said she had a gift. Often, she would sing to Jade before they both went to sleep. Slow songs about the sea and sailors who longed to go back home. When Mona first left home, that was the thing that Jade had missed the most.

Bates was sitting on his own, staring into the flames.

Around them was a place that had once been a garden

surrounded by a tumbledown wall. Beyond that were the Wetlands, dark and still, a half-moon throwing a wash of light over it. The distant sky was pitted with stars that glowed and sparkled. There were sporadic voices from the conversations at the front of the buildings and whisperings from the family inside. From the Wetlands, she could hear the occasional howl of a creature or a rustle of vegetation as something raced past.

No sound of the water rushing towards them.

Maybe this time the flood was a false alarm.

'Mary?' Bates spoke, 'What was it like? Before the first flood?'

There was a moment's silence and Old Mary frowned. Jade tensed. Her granddaddy hadn't liked to talk about past-world. Many survivors didn't. It was too painful to remember the life they had had before the water came.

'I just thought – and don't be upset about me saying this – you're an old lady. When you die your memories die with you. It would be good for me – for us – to know some of them.'

It was one of the longest things Jade had heard Bates say.

'I can barely remember,' Old Mary said.

'There must be some things . . .'

The fire flickered and Jade heard laughter coming from the other side of the farmyard. Something moved beyond the garden wall; a rabbit or fox.

'My memory's not so good . . .'

'But something about what life was like before the flood.'

'Electricals,' Old Mary said. 'The world was full of them.'

Nobody said anything. Jade noticed Rosa nodding her head in agreement.

Old Mary went on, her voice not so cheerful.

'Everything you needed was made for you. You got up in the morning and you walked into a wash-room like you've never seen. Smooth tiles and hot water and electrics everywhere. You pressed a button and the water came out and the hot air came out to dry your hair. You went for breakfast and pressed another button and the cooker came on and the water boiled and you opened the cooler door and there was enough food for you to eat for a whole week. All fresh.'

'Amazing,' Bates said.

'Everyone had their own cars or trucks and people could travel wherever they wanted to go; they didn't need lanyards. People were free then to live where they wanted. No one told them they had to stay in this area or that area.'

'Tell them about the moving stairs,' Rosa said.

Old Mary smiled and nodded to herself.

'I don't remember *why* they made them. People must have got tired walking up stairs and also, there were many high buildings.'

'So, what was it like, on the moving stairs?' Bates said, his eyes glued to old Mary.

'You had to step on them carefully. They were metal and they rose up out of the ground and you stood still and held on to a handrail. Everyone stood still, like a long queue of people moving upwards, and when you got to the top . . .'

'Yes?'

'You had to step off at just the right minute because the stairs disappeared into the machinery. You had to be quick otherwise you could stumble forward.'

Everyone laughed, trying to imagine a set of stairs that *moved*.

'What I don't get,' Bates said, 'is why it all ended.'

Nobody spoke. Mary looked pained and Rosa fiddled with the kindling, pushing it further into the flames. Bates was sitting forward waiting for an answer. Jade looked at him with surprise. Bates wasn't a great talker. He liked to listen and he rarely said anything about *his* life before he came to Peter's Town. Now he was full of questions.

'Because of the water,' Jade said. 'The water flooded everything. Well, not *everything*. Just the low lands.'

'OK, I get that. So, there are places, still now, where life is like that – with the tiles on the wall and the moving staircases?'

'Maybe. I don't know for sure,' Mary said, wearily. 'Don't forget the First Flood covered much more land before it receded. So lots of things were spoilt forever.'

'But there are places *now* where people have more things

than we do?'

Jade shrugged her shoulders. There was no need to answer. Everyone knew that life in North-Hampton and High-Town was better than life in the Wetlands. Maybe that was why older people didn't like to talk about past-world. It only made them unhappy.

'Best get some rest now,' Rosa said.

She struggled to her feet. Old Mary walked after her and they both went into the building. Bates was still looking quizzical, as if he had other questions to ask.

'We should turn in too,' Jade said. 'I want to make an early start, soon as the sun rises.'

'OK,' he shrugged, not moving. 'I'll sleep here by the door. In case anyone comes.'

Jade was unfolding her sleeping-roll when she saw Old Mary coming towards her. She was tiptoeing in an exaggerated way. She sat down on the floor next to Jade, grabbed her hand and spoke quietly.

'My dear, I didn't want to say it in front of other people, but I saw your sister in Little-Norfolk just before the Mid-Winter celebrations, six, maybe seven months ago.'

'Did you?'

'I didn't recognise her at first because she looked, well,

different. She seemed very uncared-for. Her clothes were torn and ... 'course, I didn't know her very well but whenever I saw her in Peter's Town she was so happy; always dancing and singing and dressed in flimsies and sparkles. This time, in Little-Norfolk, she was sitting very still, at the edge of the market and it didn't look as though anyone was with her. She remembered me and asked me if I'd been to Peter's Town and I told her I hadn't for a while. I asked her if she was all right and she said she was. She had a sore on her leg though and I helped clean it. I was there for a few days and I cleaned it again. On the third day I looked for her but she'd gone.'

'Oh,' Jade said.

Old Mary was squeezing her hand.

'I'll let you get to sleep. It's not the best time to tell you this, what with your granddaddy dying, but I thought you'd want to know ...'

She watched as the old woman went back to where Rosa was bedding down. The family in the corner had put out their candles and the farmhouse kitchen darkened all of a sudden. The only light was from the doorway; the hazy shine of the moon which spilled in from outside. She could see the shape of Bates, sitting, not lying, by the door. She felt a twist of anguish in her chest at the thought of Mona, alone in a strange place, injured and unkempt. Mona had always been very careful with her appearance. She'd spent hours looking at herself, painting her face, curling her hair. *I am going to be a minstrel one day,* she'd said to Jade.

But then, after the ice-winter, she'd left to earn money.

She remembered the day Mona left home. Jade had found her bed empty and a note on the kitchen table. Her granddaddy had gone all over Peter's Town looking for her. He travelled to the villages along the coast. One night went by and then another and, on the third morning, he said he was going to the Uplands to find her. He'd left Jade in the care of Rosa and some other homers. Eight days later, he returned, ruddy from the sun and gaunt, looking as if he'd not eaten for a long time. The weeks went by and no money arrived and no letter came from Mona. One day Granddaddy told Jade, *I can't think about her anymore. She's gone. She's gone forever.* So Jade made some hot sweet tea and they had stopped talking about her.

Jade reached into her back-sack and pulled out the book: *The Ballerina.* It was a thin volume with a hard cover. Mona had often caught Jade first thing in the morning as she woke. *Let's read about the ballerina,* she'd said. Sometimes Jade had turned her back, put the pillow over her head. *I don't like that book!* she'd say.

If Mona were here now, Jade would read it with her. She would.

She lay down, her head resting on her granddaddy's old shirt. It smelled of brine and salt and it reminded her of the cabin in Peter's Town, her granddaddy in the wicker chair and Mona dancing across the grass, holding a slim ribbon of bells in her hands.

TEN

JADE WOKE WITH A START. SHE'D HEARD SOMETHING. SHE lay very still, working out what it was. She tensed, pulling her knees up to her chest in case it was a rat. It took her a few seconds to remember *where* she was and she sat up, leaned on her elbows and looked around the room. It was still dark and she could only see shapes of people sleeping: the family in the corner, Rosa and Old Mary further across the floor. The back door was still hanging open.

Whatever she had heard had stopped. She lay for a few moments wondering what time it was. She was dog-tired but she was also alert, jittery, sleeping in a place she wasn't used to.

Then she heard it again. Not a rat, but some movement from outside. A cough or a sneeze. She got up quietly and went to the door and stood looking out on the darkness. In the east, the sky was lighter, so it was probably a little before dawn. The noise came from somewhere just beyond the garden wall.

She was about to walk across when she realised that Bates wasn't there. He'd said he'd sleep by the door but there was no sign of him. Possibly he had gone outside the garden to pee. She waited a moment, not wanting to embarrass him.

Then she heard a groan. The hairs stood up on the back of her neck and she stepped gingerly across the garden towards the wall.

Something moved.

'Bates?' she said in a loud whisper.

The groaning sound got louder.

Was he hurt? Had he gone out and stumbled, broken his leg or something?

It was coming from some bushes beyond the garden wall. She could see them between the gaps in the crumbling stone. She stepped across the rubble and peered into the darkness. She was about to take another step when a hand grabbed her arm and pulled her roughly to the side.

'Hey!' she said.

A piece of cloth went around her mouth and was tied roughly at the back of her head. It was tight and meant she couldn't speak. Her tongue felt like it was bunched up inside her teeth. There was a hand gripping each arm and she felt herself being dragged over the grass and stones.

'Keep up, ratty!'

She heard these words spat out three or four times and tried to pick her feet up so that she was in control of her own movements. Her captors were going at a speed but then, without warning, they came to an abrupt stop by some tall reeds on the edge of a water hole.

'I'm taking the gag off your mouth. Say a word and you'll be in the water with my foot on your back. Clear?' a voice said.

Jade nodded as she felt the tie being pulled off her face. She struggled to stand up straight. In front of her stood two boys of about her age. She could see by the pox marks on their faces that they were ferals. They were clothed in military shirts buttoned up the neck and down to the wrist, long trousers and boots. Each wore a tight scarf around his head. The only skin that was visible was on their faces and hands. The marks of the disease showed, even in the early-morning darkness.

'OK, you're not an idiot. Give us your dollar-belt.'

Jade reared up to her whole height. She straightened her shoulders and her hands curled into fists. She wasn't afraid to hit out. She'd done it enough times in Peter's Town with boys who thought they could boss her. She would fight them if she had to.

The boys looked at each other and laughed.

One of them stepped across and stood close-up to her face. Jade saw that he had a scar down the side of his cheek. It was livid and zigzagged from the corner of his eye to the top of his lip.

'See this?' the boy said, pointing to the raw-looking mark. 'This was in a fight with another rat like you. You think this looks bad, you should see what he looks like. So just hand over your dollar-belt.'

Jade hugged herself. They would have to peel her arms away before she would give up her dollars. The other boy sighed.

'Come on, ratty. There's one of you and two of us and you know we have blades. Just because I haven't got mine up at your throat, you know we have them, right? Ratty?'

'Hey, that's good,' the boy with the scar said, his hand reaching out for Jade's chain with the key. 'Give us that!'

'No,' Jade said, her hands moving up to her neck to protect it.

The other boy reached for Jade's waist and grabbed hold of her dollar-belt. He must have had a blade because he slit the fabric and it fell apart and came away in his hand. Jade looked at it in dismay but before she could say a word, the scarred boy had hold of the chain and wrenched it from her neck. She felt a second's pain as it dug into her skin then registered the *snap* as it broke and was snatched from her.

She looked on in shock as it hung from the feral's hand. She went to grab it but he jumped back.

'Thanks, ratty!' the other one said.

'Wait!'

She went after them, her feet quickening, one after the other, splashing in water, sucking up the mud; she pushed high grasses out of the way, her eyes clinging to the boys, following the noise of their laughter and jeers. But they were faster than her and she slowed up and came to a stop. Her heart was pumping and her breath was ragged as she watched them disappear into the mist.

ELEVEN

TEARS STUNG AT HER EYES AS SHE REGISTERED WHAT HAD happened. Not only had they got her dollars but they had the chain and key as well. How could she have been so stupid to come out of the farm at night, when she'd already been told that ferals were around? How could she? She began to walk back towards the buildings. Her hands were in fists and she felt a great twist of frustration inside. Now what? Getting closer, she could see that Bates was by the wall. The sight of him made her angry. She sped up and headed towards him.

'Where were you?' she hissed. 'I've been robbed by ferals.

I thought you were . . . I thought you were in trouble. I heard a noise but when I came out here there were two ferals . . .'

'You all right?' he said, looking shocked.

'They took my dollars and my granddaddy's chain that I had on round my neck.'

She was moving her feet, getting control back in her body. Her waist felt lighter without the dollar-belt and she kept feeling her neck where the chain had been.

'I was . . .'

'I thought it was you! I thought you were hurt!' she said, her voice sharp. 'Otherwise I wouldn't have come out. Where were you? You were supposed to be sleeping here!'

Bates's cap threw a block of darkness across his face.

'I went for a walk round the buildings. I stayed close to the wall. I just wanted to see who was here.'

'I thought it was *you* out there. That's why I came out!'

'Sorry. They didn't hurt you though?'

She shook her head and thought about the boy with the jagged scar. It sat like a bolt of lightning on his face.

'Which ferals were they?'

'They had military stuff on. Covered up, of course, but I could see the scars . . .'

'Marines. They live in boats about ten kilometres along from the pontoon-crossing. They only come on to land to get stuff. They keep themselves to themselves.'

'Except when they want something!' Jade, said, angrily.

'They took your granddaddy's chain. That's bad.'

'I've got to get it back.'

'Is it worth dollars?'

In a way, it was. She needed the key to give to Charlie Diamond. It was important that she had it. It was also the last thing her granddaddy had given her.

'Yes, no. It's sentimental.'

'Because you loved your granddaddy?'

Bates was looking straight at her. His words threw her. It was such a direct, personal question that Jade didn't know what to say.

'Yes, I suppose.'

'You're lucky. Loving another person is really good . . .'

In spite of herself, Jade felt bad for Bates. For a second, she forgot she'd just been held against her will and robbed. She wanted to put her hand out and comfort him in some way, but he was all sharp angles and clenched teeth.

'Did you not know *any* parent?'

Bates shook his head.

'How did you live? How were you looked after?'

'I wasn't. I had help. I lived with a couple of families for a while. I worked for a fisherman. He died though, and I just kept moving.'

Jade didn't know what to say. It was the first time he'd said anything about his past. She was sorry for Bates but, at the moment, she had her own troubles.

'I have to get my stuff back from the ferals.'

As she said it, she knew how useless it sounded. It was all brag. The ferals lived in groups. Even if she could find the boys, there was no way she could make them give her the key and the money back. She swore using words her granddaddy had told her not to say. She knew it was hopeless.

'I know that camp,' Bates said, 'and I know one of the ferals. A boy called Samson. I can talk to him.'

'That's against the law. *No one* is supposed to talk to ferals.'

Bates shrugged his shoulders. Jade was surprised. Bates's past was more colourful than she could have imagined.

'Do you think you can help me get my stuff back?'

'Sure. The boy I know is important there. I can ask him. Explain how the stuff is valuable to you . . .'

She felt a spark of hope. If Bates knew someone it might all be OK. She looked around and saw that the sky had lightened; it was almost dawn. A couple of hours to the estuary and, once she got her belongings back they could head for the pontoon-crossing.

'What do you want to do?' he said.

Could it really work?

She had to try because there was no other way.

TWELVE

THE FARMHOUSE WAS COMPLETELY SILENT AS THEY GOT THEIR stuff together. Walking quietly out, Jade tapped Old Mary on the shoulder and told her they were leaving. She didn't explain what had happened because she didn't want any fuss. She said she'd see them later at North-Hampton.

They went off the main track for the pontoon-crossing because the feral camp was further east, closer to the sea. Bates was leading. Jade began to worry about the flooding and as they went on, the ground seemed to be more broken up with waterways and pools; the earth beneath her feet felt soggy. They really should be heading *away* from the water, not towards it.

She had to get that key back though.

'Don't worry about the water. There are boats all over the place where the Marines are,' Bates said, as if he'd read her mind.

They passed groups of derelict buildings and warehouses. The roads that led up to them had lost their edges where vegetation had taken over. Now and then, there were past-world road signs with numbers: A14, A12, M11. The poles that held them high had creeper-weed growing up them. In the distance, they saw a truck heading back into the Wetlands and Jade wondered if it was the one that was going back for Rosa.

'Much further?' she called.

'We should come to the estuary soon. Then it's a couple of kilometres.'

After a while they stopped to take a drink from the water bags. Jade could see a liquid haze a little further on and she guessed it was the estuary. Straight ahead was a promontory where the land raised a little. There were buildings on it.

'Fisherman's huts. It was where I lived for a while,' Bates said, 'but the fishermen left when chemicals ate up the water. The ferals stayed though.'

'Was that when you got to know Samson?'

He nodded and Jade screwed her face up.

'Weren't you worried you might catch something from him?'

'That's a myth. Once the disease has gone it's not infectious. Look at me!'

She stared at Bates. Even though he was small and not well-nourished, his skin was smooth. He also looked happier than she had seen before.

'Or are you worried that I might have it and pass it on to you? Too late now!'

They walked around the abandoned buildings. The shore of the estuary slipped away and the water nearby had an oily sheen on it. There were some rowboats and canoes stuck in the reeds, turned half sideways. There was a vague smell, like the cans of diesel that were sometimes carried in the rear of a truck.

'Where is the camp?'

'Out there,' Bates said.

He pointed out into the water. There was a still mist on it and Jade couldn't see anything much.

'Stand behind me. Look over my shoulder. If you concentrate there, where my finger is, you'll see some shapes. That's where they are.'

She stood behind him and focused on where he was pointing. There were some dark blocks on the estuary.

'In the middle of the water? What is it, an island?'

'Kind of. It's an island made of boats. They're all tied together, about forty of them, tethered so that you can walk from one boat to the other. It's their camp. They call it Little-Venice.'

'How weird!'

'Not weird. It's genius. Remember they're not allowed to live on the land or mix with us. Plus, they live on the top of the water. If the water level rises then their boats rise.'

'But why Little-Venice?'

'There was a place, in past-world, called Venice. It was a city where the homes were built on a hundred or more small islands. They were linked with solid bridges.'

Jade had never seen a solid bridge. She had never been further than North-Hampton.

'They're pretty clever, the ferals, if you ask me,' Bates said.

'Yeah, very clever to creep on to the land and rob people.'

'I know that's not good but they have no other way of living. They're not allowed to come on the land to farm or live. They fish but you can't exist on fish alone.'

Jade frowned. She had enough of her own problems. She did not want to start feeling sorry for anyone. She thought of the two boys who had come in the early hours of the morning and taken her stuff. She kept picturing the red scar on the boy's already disease-damaged face.

'So how do we get out there?'

'We take a boat. I know where they keep them.'

'And when we get there, what happens then?'

'I'll speak to my friend.'

'Are you sure? What if the boys who robbed me are there? And how do we find this Samson?'

'So many questions! It's easy,' he said, 'I'll just whistle for him.'

THIRTEEN

FOUR BOATS WERE HIDDEN IN CLUMPS OF REEDS. HOLDING their bags up, Jade and Bates splashed through the water, climbed on to one and used a paddle to push it away from the shore. They glided through the ripples, silently. It was mid-morning yet mist lay on the surface like flimsy. The tide was coming in gently and it wasn't hard to paddle against it. Here the estuary was wide like a lake, not a river, and Little-Venice, the feral camp, was in the middle.

'I lived there for a few weeks after my fisherman died. Then I left and came to Peter's Town.'

She was learning more about Bates's past. Perhaps it was one of the reasons he had been reluctant to talk about it.

Doing anything with ferals was strictly forbidden.

They paddled on. Even though they could see the shape of the camp on the water it seemed to take an age to get any closer. The 'boat' was a cross between a raft and a canoe. It came to a point at the front, but there were low sides and the water dribbled over as they got further into the estuary.

'Cup it out with your hands,' Bates said.

She did so, flinging it over the side. They seemed to move more quickly. After a while, Bates spoke.

'Frank told me about your sister, Mona.'

She was surprised. She stopped what she was doing.

'He did?'

'He talked about her a lot. Well, in the last couple of weeks. Ever since that day when the ryder came.'

She thought of Spike, the ryder. They weren't friends exactly, but she'd often returned home and found him sitting cross-legged on the porch, his silver bi-cycle leaning against the wall of the cabin, a cup of hot sweet tea in his hands.

'It was like he'd *just* remembered her. Not exactly . . . but you know what I mean?'

Jade wondered if it was the day that Spike had brought him the card for the Butterfly Palace. She couldn't remember exactly what day that had been. She'd seen Spike a few times in the weeks before the sirens started. That wasn't unusual. He did trips for many of the homers. He was reliable and trusted. If homers gave him things to sell, he came back with the right amount of dollars, less his fee.

Bates was still talking.

'Frank didn't exactly say what had happened to her. It was just about when she was young. He said she was the silly one and you were sensible. She was always daydreaming but you had your feet firmly on the ground.'

That was true. Mona found it hard to work out how many dollars they needed for food or how to sort out the washing or the cupboards. She had no idea of *real* things, but she could sing and dance and make people laugh.

'She left us to go and find work,' Jade said, 'after the ice-winter.'

'Oh.'

'It was too cold to dive, too cold to do anything. People in the village ran out of fuel and there was hardly any food. Granddaddy was still well then but there was nothing he could do.'

Jade remembered it as a terrible time. The dogs left the village and the rats came. She lay in bed and heard them scrabbling on the roof of their cabin. In the morning, as soon as it was daylight, she would see them out of the corner of her eye, racing across the window ledge.

'There were places by the estuary that froze over,' Bates said. 'Nobody could fish.'

'Some of the alms-workers came to the village to help. They talked about farms in the Uplands that needed labour.

As soon as the weather changed, Mona said she was going to go and find work there. She said she'd lie about her age and that she'd send money back. I wasn't to tell Granddaddy until she'd gone. I didn't. Many a time since then I wish I had.'

'Did she get work? Did she send money back?'

Jade shook her head.

'Her real ambition was to join the minstrels.'

Jade had only ever seen the minstrels from a distance; their brightly coloured trucks and caravans; the flags and banners that fluttered in the breeze when they moved about the Wetlands. They went further afield: North-Hampton, High-Town and the rest of the Uplands.

'At first, Granddaddy thought that's what she'd done. He was sure that she'd run off to join them. But we saw them at North-Hampton the last time the sirens sounded and they said they'd never seen her.'

'You don't think . . . that something happened to her?'

She paused. The water was still coming into the boat. She started to scoop it out again. She considered telling Bates what her granddaddy had told her, but she remembered his words. *Don't tell anyone, even the boy.*

'I don't know.'

'You miss her. I can tell.'

Jade nodded but didn't speak. Bates looked as though he was going to say something else but then stopped himself.

She *wanted* to talk about her sister. She would have *loved* to chat about her, but Granddaddy's instructions were weighing heavily on her. And she still had to get the key back and get to Monks' Alley and Charlie Diamond's shop.

She scooped the water out more vigorously and they went along in silence.

They moved forward, towards the middle of the estuary. Jade could now see the outline of the feral village. The tide was quickening, she could tell; it was harder to paddle, to keep the boat on course. Little-Venice was emerging from the mist, becoming clearer and more substantial. She could make out numbers of boats side by side, rocking on the water, maybe twenty or more. Getting closer, she could see that there were others behind them, all different sizes. In the centre was a bigger boat. It rose up above the others; she could see its funnel. The smaller boats around were tethered to it by thick ropes. Other boats were tied to them. It *was* like a floating village.

'Won't they see us coming?'

'They'll recognise me so there won't be any trouble.'

'How come the wardens don't get rid of the camp? They must know it's here.'

'It suits the wardens for people to have someone to hate, to blame everything on, to be fearful of. That means we don't hate *them.* That's what Will told me. My fisherman, before he died.'

She remembered that Bates had denied living with *William* at Shallow Creek. Was Will, Bates's fisherman, the same person?

Coming up to the camp she could see how the whole village undulated, some smaller boats on the outside rocking more than the sturdier ones.

'We head for that,' Bates said.

He pointed to a place on the eastern most part of the village where there was a floating dock that had old vehicle tyres all around it. Standing on top of it was a young man dressed from head to foot and wearing a hooded top.

'It's OK. He knows me.'

They stopped paddling and Bates used his hands to steer the boat towards the dock. Coming closer, Jade braced herself as they hit the rubber tyres with a bump. The feral reached down and snatched up a bundle of rope that was stuffed into the V at the front of the boat. He tied it over the top of one of the tyres. Bates held his hand out and the feral gripped it as he jumped off on to the dock. Then Bates turned round and held his hand out for Jade. She was relieved. She hadn't wanted to make *physical* contact with the feral, whatever Bates said about them not being infectious.

'You back for good?' the feral said.

'Not sure. Maybe. Going to see Samson.'

'You know where he is.'

'Sure. Thanks.'

Bates pulled her arm and led her off the dock on to a long boat that had a walkway down the side. Half-way along, they stepped off on to another that was sandwiched up to it, then another and another. She'd been wrong about the amount of boats. There were many more than she first thought, some at right angles to the main body, as if they were little alleyways stretching off. In the middle was the big boat and she could see its steel funnel and raised bridge. On the side, its name had been painted in large bold lettering: *The Navigator.*

'That's usually where the market is,' Bates said.

There were some people on the deck looking over at them, but Bates turned away and stepped on to the first of a line of long thin vessels all roped end-to-end like a string of sausages. They walked quickly along the smaller boats, which rocked gently at each footstep. When they got to the third one along, Bates knocked on the door quietly. Then he started to whistle like a bird. No one answered so he did it again. This time the whistling was louder and longer.

A door opened and a head popped out.

'What's going on?'

A boy leaned around the doorway. He had long fair hair and smooth skin, no sign of any pockmark or blemish. Jade was puzzled.

'I need your help,' Bates said.

'I thought you might turn up again. Who's the rat?'

She bristled. *Rat* was an insult to people who lived in the Wetlands.

'She's my friend. Her name's Jade. Don't call her rat. She already hates the ferals. I want you to meet her and change her mind.'

'You better come in then,' Samson said, standing to one side so that they could both enter his boat.

Jade looked around at the surrounding water, the tide moving more quickly now. She wasn't comfortable here but she needed to get her things back. She bent her shoulders and lowered her head and went into the boat.

FOURTEEN

THE CABIN WAS TINY, WITH JUST ENOUGH ROOM FOR A BED AND a chair. Jade stood awkwardly while Bates told Samson what had happened when she'd been robbed. She looked Samson over. He had on a vest-shirt which was baggy but didn't cover the pockmarks on his forearms. Jade couldn't pull her eyes away from looking at the scars, the remains of the pox. His face and neck were clear. If she just focused on them, Samson looked like any other Wetlands homer.

'What did these boys look like?' Samson said to Jade, irritated, as if somehow *Jade* were to blame.

'One of them had a jagged scar from his eye to his lip.'

'That's Cory. She's a *girl*, not a boy!'

He shook his head as if Jade was stupid.

'A girl? How was I supposed to know?'

'Never mind, ratty . . .'

'Don't call her that . . .' Bates said.

'Cory knows we don't steal from kids. That's a rule. Adults are fair game. But not kids and specially not kids on their way to the dykes at North-Hampton.'

'You do have a moral code then.'

'I don't expect you to understand, ratty . . .'

Jade squared up, angry now. She hadn't been threatened, robbed and come all this way to be insulted as well.

'Samson! I asked you not to call her that. Don't you think she's been through enough?' Bates said.

'Sorry, sorry.'

Just then, the floor of the boat seemed to see-saw up and down, as though it had bumped over something in the water. Samson was startled by it.

'Tide's coming much stronger than before.'

'Is this the deluge?'

'Don't know. It's definitely pushing harder than any of the high tides I've seen in the last few months.'

Jade was frustrated. The water was coming and she had to get her stuff back and get to North-Hampton. She looked straight at Samson.

'Will you help me? The dykes close at North-Hampton at sixteen hours.'

Samson nodded.

'I'll do it but there's something you have to do for me.'

'What?'

'I want to come into North-Hampton. There are meds I have to get. There'll be so many people around I'll be able to get about without being noticed.'

'But you're not allowed . . .'

'I can pass for normal. Especially if I'm travelling with you.'

'It's illegal for us to help you.'

Samson held his hands out.

'I give you something. You help me.'

'That's OK. We can do that, Jade?'

Bates was frowning at her. The floor they were standing on lifted and then subsided.

'I don't know if it's just an especially high tide or whether it's the flood, but you need to make a decision,' Samson said.

Jade didn't know what to do. Punishment for helping ferals was being sent to Landfill. She'd heard of people who had to spend years there, digging all day long, pulling out miscellanies from past-world. Back-breaking work and no pay.

'Come on, Jade. We haven't got that long until the dykes close.'

She *needed* that key to take to Charlie Diamond. She pushed Landfill out of her mind.

'All right. OK. You can come in with us.'

'Good,' Samson said, pulling a shirt on. 'Now let's get your stuff back from Cory.'

FIFTEEN

THEY WALKED BACK TOWARDS THE CONGLOMERATION OF BOATS, *The Navigator* sitting proud and high in the middle. Jade took care to step from one to the other, holding on to the ropes that hung from each vessel. She kept glancing around at the estuary. The water looked like it was in a hurry to get somewhere. She could hear it slapping against the sides of the boats. Up ahead, Samson seemed unperturbed, stepping lightly from vessel to vessel. There were more ferals out now, perhaps alerted by the swift tide, peering into the distance.

Samson stopped alongside a tiny, scruffy boat that had letters painted on it.

'You two head over to the back dock. You remember where it is, Bates?'

He nodded.

'What about my stuff?' Jade said.

'All in good time, ratty.'

'Oh, I give up . . .' Bates said.

'Bates, get on the engine-boat. Here's the starter. Get it ready. I'll be along soon. Remember, it has to be powered up and ready to go.'

'OK,' Bates said, a small piece of shaped metal in his hand.

Samson pushed against the door of the cabin with his foot and went inside. Bates nudged Jade in a different direction.

'How do we know we can trust him?' Jade said.

'He's my friend. I can vouch for him. Anyway, he needs us to get into North-Hampton.'

He walked ahead. They were skirting *The Navigator*. After walking round the stern, they came to another dock. There were small crafts lined up, tied to the rubber tyres that laced the edge of the platform.

'This way.'

At the far edge was a red boat. It stood out from the others because it had an engine attached to the rear.

'Come on,' Bates said, stepping off the dock.

Jade followed him on to the boat, holding on for balance. She sat down and watched as he pulled out the piece of metal that was in a warped Z shape. He inserted one end of the Z into the engine and used the other end to turn it. The engine gave a shudder and then rattled and rumbled into life. She looked past Bates towards the row of boats that they had come along and in the distance she thought she could see a figure running towards them.

'That's it,' Bates said.

The engine was humming and Bates began to undo the rope that was tied to the rubber tyre. Jade looked back and saw that the figure *was* running towards them. It was Samson and there was another person coming behind, running and jumping from boat to boat.

'Help me,' Bates said.

The rope that was holding the boat to the floating dock was long, enormously long. It lay in a great snake in the boat, tangling his feet.

'Help me push a little,' Bates shouted above the noise of the engine.

She leaned across to the row of tyres and pushed her weight against them. The boat moved out from the side even though Bates still had the end of the rope hooked on to another tyre.

Samson was close now and behind him Jade could see Cory, the *girl* with the zig-zag scar. Cory was running fast, leaping from boat to boat. She had no scarf on her head and Jade could see brown springy corkscrew curls.

'Push it out,' Samson cried.

Bates waited for a few seconds then pulled the end of the rope off the tyre and the boat began to move backwards, pulled by the hurrying tide.

Cory caught up with Samson. She shouted angrily and grabbed his arm. He tumbled forward.

'Hold the boat steady!' Jade said.

Cory was lying half on top of Samson's back, pummelling him with her fist. She looked up for a moment and saw them. She was shouting things that Jade couldn't quite hear.

'What's going to happen?' Jade said. 'Should we tie up and get out and help?'

Bates shook his head but she could see that he was holding the rudder in such a way that the boat was not moving more than a metre from the dock.

Samson threw Cory off and she stumbled backwards and fell on to a nearby boat. He came towards the dock but in seconds she was there behind him.

'Push the boat out!' he called again.

Bates let the rudder go and the boat drifted away from the dock. Jade was sure Samson wouldn't make it. Cory was close behind him and had grabbed hold of his shirt. There was a sound of tearing but Samson didn't stop; he made an almighty jump into the air. The spring in Samson's jump propelled him off the dock and into the boat. He tumbled on to the skein of rope, curled up and rolled on his side. The boat rocked dangerously and Jade had to hold on to the side. Just then, Bates pulled a wire from the engine and the boat shot away from the dock, leaving Cory behind, shouting, her fist in the air, holding a strip of Samson's shirt.

SIXTEEN

THE BOAT CUT THROUGH THE ESTUARY RAPIDLY. SAMSON
pulled himself up to a sitting position. He'd taken off his
torn shirt and discarded it. He was cradling his arm and his
face was cracked with pain. Jade could see that he'd landed
badly and was injured.

'Where to, Skipper?' Bates said, steering the boat.

'North-Hampton, First Officer!'

They both laughed and Jade looked away.

'Injuries?'

Samson shook his head and continued feeling his
shoulder. He grimaced and moved his arm in a circular
motion.

'Nothing's broke,' he said. 'Just bruised, maybe.'

'Can I have my stuff?' Jade said, her hand out.

Samson looked at her with disdain.

'Thanks for your concern about my welfare, ratty.'

Bates sighed.

'I just want my stuff back. I didn't ask anyone to steal it from me!'

'But you did ask me to get it back for you!'

'Which is only right,' Jade said, 'seeing as your lot took it from me!'

'Point taken.'

Samson sat back, still massaging his shoulder.

'You can have it back when we get through the dykes at North-Hampton.'

'What?'

'I have to be sure that you'll go through the entry gates with me. I know *he* will. He's my friend. Trouble is, he doesn't look that respectable.'

'Thanks!' Bates said.

'You looked better before you shaved your hair off.'

Bates shrugged and pulled the peak of his cap down further.

'How do I even know you've got my stuff?'

Samson sighed and then put his hand into a pocket and pulled out Jade's dollar belt.

'Where's my chain . . . ?'

Samson upended the purse and the dollars fell out, followed by the chain and the key. They all lay on the deck of the boat. Jade picked up the chain and key. The chain was broken from where it had been pulled off her neck.

'What's to stop me taking it now?' Jade said.

'Nothing,' Samson said, 'but I'll toss you over the side. You can swim to the riverbank but you won't get to the pontoon-crossing in time to get into North-Hampton.'

She knew that Samson was right. Frustrated, she nodded and Samson picked up her things, put them back into the dollar belt and shoved it back into the pocket of his trousers. Jade focused on his arms, which were pitted with scars.

'Why didn't you get any scars on your face?' she said.

'Who knows? There's a few people in my village that didn't. Good luck? Or maybe bad luck?'

'Good luck, surely, if you can pass for normal.'

'I am *normal*. I just happen to have had a disease.'

Jade didn't answer. Ever since she could remember, people had talked about ferals in a fearful way. They'd got the disease because they were a bad lot to start off with; the disease just made them worse. They were embittered, jealous of normal people. They were keen to infect others or take their possessions, so people should avoid having anything to do with them.

'I'm the same as you – in here. I was just unlucky enough to get ill.'

Samson pointed at his chest. Jade knew that he meant that he was the same in his heart. But was that possible? People who lived such a different life to her? Who depended on robbery to get by? Jade didn't answer. She turned away and looked towards the shore. The estuary was narrowing, the banks becoming more overgrown with trees and bushes, obscuring the view of the Wetlands.

'Where do we stop?' Jade said.

'As close to the pontoon-crossing as we can without anyone seeing us. There's a place where I can moor the boat,' Samson said.

The boat held its course, carried along by the speed of the incoming tide. Samson was talking quietly to Bates and he was smiling at him as if they shared a secret. Jade felt hurt. Bates had been *her* friend for the past weeks.

She thought of Kris, the girl who she'd been close to in Peter's Town. They'd sat together for some school classes. They'd liked each other immediately and had walked home in the afternoon, linking arms, whispering things to each other. Sometimes Kris would stay at her house until her aunty called for her. Then one day, some months ago, she came to the cabin and said she was leaving the next morning to live in another village far away. Jade had waved to her from the village square. Then she was gone and Jade no longer had anyone to share her stories with. Bates had turned up not long after that.

Samson laughed out loud at something and slapped Bates on his back.

The boat moved towards the shore-line. Up ahead, in the far distance, Jade could see a dark shape across the river. It was the pontoon-crossing. She looked up at the sky at the position of the sun. It was past the middle of the day, maybe fourteen hours. Rosa and Old Mary should have crossed by now.

On the shore, further up was an electric-pylon. It was one of the ones that was still standing upright, untouched by any of the floods. The wires that had once attached it to the others were gone, stolen by scavengers. She was surprised that so much of the pylon was still there. Many of them had been cut apart and used in the villages round the Wetlands, like the water tower in Peter's Town.

The boat pulled up alongside it.

'Help me!' Samson said, standing up, getting his balance. 'Pick up the rope.'

Jade reached across to the skein and tried to lift it. It was heavy so she got on to her knees and hefted it up into her arms. Samson took a length and tied it loosely round his shoulder. Jade held the rope up as Samson looped it over and over until most of the rope hung on him.

Bates stopped the motor. The boat was still moving though, carried by the brisk tide.

'Use the paddle to steer into those bushes,' he hissed.

Jade picked up a paddle and began to manoeuvre the boat into the bank of the river. She could feel the power of the water pulling the boat away but she kept going, helped by Bates who used the second paddle on the other side. The base of the electric-pylon was in among the grasses. As soon as the boat went aground, Samson jumped out of it and began to climb up the leg of the pylon. At each step he stopped and allowed the rope to uncurl and hang down. Even with his bruised shoulder he was fit. Jade wondered why he was going to such a height to tie up the boat.

Then she knew.

If the flood came and the boat was tethered to something low it would be submerged. This was in case the water rose dramatically; the boat would simply float on top of it. It was a smart thing to do. Bates was right. The ferals weren't stupid.

Samson was tying the rope to one of the steel arms. Then he began to slither down the structure, gathering speed as he went. In moments he was beside them.

'Now we head for the crossing,' he said. 'And then into North-Hampton.'

He was wiping his forehead with the back of his hand.

'What if someone sees your arms and that hand?' Jade said, pointing to his right hand, which had scars near the wrist.

'I can wear my shirt,' he said, picking it up from the deck. 'It's ripped, though.'

'It's not like I have a choice,' Samson said, looking irritated.

Jade thought for a moment.

'I have something you can wear. It belonged to my granddaddy. It's big so the cuffs will cover your hands.'

She dragged her granddaddy's shirt out of her back-sack and handed it to Samson.

'Sure?' he said.

'Sure,' Jade said. 'But I'll have it back afterwards.'

'OK, ratty. It's a deal.'

NORTH-HAMPTON

SEVENTEEN

THEY STEPPED ON TO THE PONTOON-CROSSING. BEHIND THEM were the Wetlands, flat and waterlogged; in front of them were slopes and hills and solid dry earth.

Jade immediately felt the pontoon-crossing sway beneath her feet. Bates stumbled a little and righted himself. Over the side, Jade could see the water racing past. Even in the short time since they'd tied the boat to the pylon, the tide had strengthened. Bobbing along in it were plastix, thousands of them. She looked back at the south banks of the estuary and saw the waves frothing at the edges, a surge or two away from spilling over. The land on the north side went gradually upwards towards North-Hampton. She quickened her step, wondering how much longer until the water would engulf everything.

It wasn't possible to see the town clearly. It was hidden by the dyke; a solid wall erected around the buildings. It was a bulky and uneven structure that had been constructed with anything and everything: old vehicles and dead machinery; rubble and cement and bricks; plastix and cubes of past-world debris from landfill. It was high and thick and ugly, but it kept out the water. The only beautiful thing about the dyke was the giant metal gates in the centre.

Most people walked quietly, although some children were making noises or calling out to each other. Dotted along the sides of the bridge were wardens, dressed from head to toe in black; pale faced men and women with long faces. Around their necks hung the white lanyards that wardens from North-Hampton had to wear. They seemed to be staring into space, but every now and again their eyes flicked here and there, like birds looking for worms. Beyond the bridge was a line of wardens at tables filtering people through.

The bridge seemed to tip to one side and Jade had to hold on in case she fell. There were shouts and people were pointing at the water. She looked over the side as the river seemed to swell and then disappear under the floor of the bridge. She hurried on and sensed Bates and Samson were just behind her. Finally, after what seemed like a long time, the three of them stepped off the pontoon-crossing and on to firm land. It felt strange and Jade wanted to stop for a moment and get her bearings, but they were chivvied along towards the line of tables. She reached the front of a queue and faced a woman who sat stiffly with a clipboard. She was wearing a black outfit with a white lanyard round her neck. Her hair was pulled back off her face and she looked at them with irritation.

'Village?' she said.

'Peter's Town.'

'Three of you?' she said.

'Yes.'

'East Bay Camp. Pull your sleeves up. Have your arms ready for stamping.'

Jade felt Samson stiffen. Further along the tables a warden was placing a rubber stamp on the forearms of the homers. There were half a dozen people lined up in front of them. This was new. Whenever she'd come to North-Hampton with her granddaddy, no one had tried to stamp them.

'What do I do?' Samson whispered, looking stricken.

She didn't know. There were only three people in front of them now.

Samson swore and Jade glanced down at his arms, covered up to the fingers with her granddaddy's shirt. She got an idea.

'Do the cuffs of the shirt up tightly,' she hissed. 'Leave the talking to me.'

It was a male warden who was doing the stamping. Jade

steeled herself and put her arm out when she got up to him. The warden didn't make eye contact with her, just placed a circular stamp on to a pad of ink and then pressed it to the skin on her arm. A red *W* sat there. The man began to do the same thing again but when he saw that Samson's shirt hadn't been rolled back he stopped and looked up at him in exasperation.

'What's going on? Roll your sleeve up! There's more to come after you. I haven't got all day.'

Samson seemed to freeze.

'Come on!'

Jade pointed to Samson's arms.

'My brother got burned in a fire. His arms are blistered and painful. He can barely move them and he can't leave them open to the air in case of infection.'

'What fire?'

'In our village. Peter's Town. There was a fire in the Worship-Hall and my brother ran in to save some children. You can ask anyone from there,' Jade added, knowing full well that there was no one from Peter's Town around them now.

A discordant sound started, a klaxon tolling loudly. It must have been a warning alarm for people to get through the gates. Homers in the queue started to look around fearfully, as if they were afraid the water was going to sweep them away at any moment. The warden's attention was momentarily diverted. Then he looked back to Samson.

'What am I supposed to do then? Boy?' he said. 'Where do I stamp you?'

'You could put the stamp on his neck. At the front so that everyone can see,' Jade said.

'That's most irregular. Most irregular.'

The queue was building up behind them, people waiting to go into the town. There were children crying and some adults shouting crossly for them to get on with it. The klaxon sounded as though it was inside Jade's head.

The warden was gripping the stamp. A female warden shouted about getting the queue moving. A small child was shrieking.

'You're right. Maybe he should roll up his sleeve,' Jade said. 'There might be blood from the broken blisters though . . .'

Jade felt her heart thumping as she put her fingers on the cuffs of the shirt as if she was about to undo it.

'No, no, no,' the warden said. 'Lean your head over this way. Come on, ratty. I haven't got all day.'

Jade pursed her lips. Now Samson knew what it was like to be insulted. The man stamped Samson's neck with some irritable force.

'Move on, move on.'

They walked on, Jade out in front. The others were coming up behind her. Their voices were light, full of relief after the near-miss.

'Where's my stuff?'she said with her hand out.

Samson seemed to pull himself together, his face becoming serious.

'Right.'

He held out her dollar belt.

'Thanks.'

She took it and marched off up the path towards the town. Samson and Bates walked a little behind her and she could hear them talking quietly. She came up towards the gate and saw a large sign attached to the wall of the dyke. It was high up but the print was large and bold. She hadn't seen it on her last visit to the town.

WARNING

Any homers who contracted the virus *Variola major* or *Variola minor* (Smallpox) are STRICTLY FORBIDDEN to enter North-Hampton or High-Town.

Diseased persons will be arrested and judged by the High-Wardens.

Penalty will be a most Merciful Death.

She felt her shoulders knot up as she read it. She already

knew the rules but it was hard to read them in black and white so soon after she'd lied her way past the wardens. It was as if everyone knew that she'd just broken the law.

Samson and Bates both glanced at the sign but neither said anything. Samson's smile faded and Bates pulled the peak of his cap down. The three of them walked towards the gates in silence.

EIGHTEEN

AS JADE STRODE AHEAD TOWARDS THE EAST BAY CAMP, THERE was an almighty noise; a creaking, like machinery moving slowly. In among it was a dreadful scraping sound.

The gates of the town were beginning to close.

Many people stood still for a moment, looking over at them. The doors famously moved slowly, centimetre by centimetre. Her granddaddy had told her that they took an hour to shut completely. There were still homers coming through, some breaking into a run as if the doors were about to slam on their ankles.

The noise would continue for the next sixty minutes.

Jade moved on, keen to get away from it and find some

others from Peter's Town. The encampment was huge, covering most of the green space in the town. Some giant tents had been erected by North-Hampton Committees. There was a free food-hall and wash facilities, as well as a lot of sleeping space. There were other motley tents brought by homers themselves and set up in designated areas. It wasn't the first time this had happened. Twice in the last couple of years, the Wetlanders had been called into North-Hampton. Once they'd been sent home within hours and the second time they'd stayed one day before the tide started to recede. This time it didn't seem like a false alarm.

Jade was zig-zagging between the tents, side-stepping tiny homesteads, edging around cooking pots, small children and animals. She quickly found some homers she knew and they pointed to one of the largest tents where others were staying. She soon saw Rosa in a corner, near the main opening.

'We wondered what had happened to you!' Rosa said, grabbing Jade's arm and pulling her into the space, 'You must stay with us, there's room. And for Bates.'

Rosa had clearly been tending to people because she was now wearing her armband as well as her red cross. No doubt she had gone about the camp to find out who was sick as soon as she got there.

'There's room for your *other* friend as well,' Rosa said, looking behind her.

Jade turned around and saw Bates and Samson were coming up.

'Thanks, Rosa. Where's Mary?' she said.

'She's gone looking for herbs. There are some homers who have fevers in another tent. We have our hands full.'

Samson and Bates had reached them.

'This is Samson,' Jade said, 'he's a friend of Bates.'

Rosa nodded pleasantly.

'He is welcome,' she said. 'You're all welcome.'

After washing and getting something to eat, Jade left them.

The main encampment was on a sloping area of grassland, between the dyke and the built-up part of the town. It was a place where ball games were sometimes played and races were held. The grassland went right round the southern and eastern edges of the town. After that the dense wall hugged the built-up areas. The dyke circled the town like protective arms.

Jade walked up the slope towards an arch and then looked back. She had never seen the town as full as it was now. She surveyed the tents, the bunting strung between them, the flags sticking up. It was packed and busy, people moving around, children running here and there.

Mona had loved coming to North-Hampton. Jade

remembered her talking about it incessantly, taking ages to get ready, telling her friends at the play-park that they were going. As Mona got older she would ask their granddaddy if she could go to the music-pit and listen to the players. Jade would always want to go as well but Mona would shake her head and flounce off. She'd come back hours later with her face flushed, carrying some piece of flimsy and an ornament that she would give Jade – a painted pebble or glass bead. Jade had collected these and kept them in a box under her bed. Months after Mona had gone, Jade had returned the pebbles to the sea.

The gates had finally closed but there were still odd grinding noises coming from them. It put Jade on edge and she wondered about the water and whether it had come up to the dyke. There didn't seem to be an air of panic.

She went through the arch.

The town was so different from where she lived. There was hardly any sky. She could only see it in oblongs and squares above the roofs. The buildings were from past-world, her granddaddy had told her. They were tall and solid and threw shadows everywhere, so it always seemed like it was late in the day. The smells jumped out at her: frying food, engine-puff, paint, tar, chemicals. Now and again there was the smell of bread cooking; big ballooning loaves or small dough-balls, fried and dipped in sugar.

She and her granddaddy often headed for the north end

of the town. He had shown her a secret place that he'd found years before when he spent some time building sections of the dyke. It was a staircase that was no longer used. There were chains across the bottom but they were easy to slip under. *Come up and see the Crow's Nest,* he'd said. They'd headed up a set of spiral steps, which got narrower nearer the top and then there was an metal gate to open. Once at the top, they were standing on an old builder's platform which overlooked a portion of the dyke. Looking over the side they could see the vast Wetlands spread out before them. *It's like we're in a ship*, her granddaddy said. *A crow's nest.*

Then they would look beyond the dyke at the northern end of the town to the road that led up to High-Town. It was two kilometres away but it might as well have been on the other side of the world because Jade had never seen it.

Now, down on the ground, noises came from everywhere. The vehicles beeped and vroomed; snatches of recorded-music came from windows and shops; there was shouting and the sound of alarms coming from somewhere.

There was no birdsong, no squawking of chickens or dogs barking. No sound of the waves washing against the beach or slapping against the jetty. No distant cry of child or goat. Here in North-Hampton she wasn't going to hear the boats creaking as they shifted on the water, nor would anyone hear the musical sound of the chimes tinkling as the wind fidgeted with them.

There were so many people in one place. They walked on the pavements or stood outside shops; they worked on vehicles or sold food from stalls. The orange bibs of the ryders flashed here and there as their bi-cycles or engine-bikes turned down alleys or slid along the pavement. Many pedestrians had the blue uniforms of the domestics and were heading home after a day working in High-Town, where they were employed to clean houses or wash laundry or tidy up flower-gardens. Tomorrow morning, they would go to the red-bus garage and back into High-Town again.

It was so different to her world and she didn't like it much.

'Oi, you, girl!'

A voice shouted from behind her. She spun round and saw one of the wardens standing a few metres away. It was a woman. She was all in black, wearing the white lanyard around her neck. She had on metal eye-glasses.

'You're a Wetlander, right?' she said. 'Let me see your stamp.'

Jade pushed her sleeve up and held out her arm.

'Why are you hanging around here?'

'I'm just going to see a friend of my granddaddy's.'

The woman frowned at her. Jade recognised her then. She'd been at the gate earlier when they were getting stamped.

'We don't want any criminal activity in the town, or anywhere else for that matter.'

Jade felt herself going red. She had brought a feral into

North-Hampton and she planned to go into High-Town. Both of these things were highly illegal.

'No theft. No loitering around and no damaging anything. I know how you Wetlanders can be. Right?'

'Right.'

'Off you go. Then get back to the camp. I don't want to see you walking round in the dark, right?'

'OK.'

Jade headed off in the direction of Monks' Alley. As she was walking, she could feel the warden's eyes on her back, but she didn't look round.

NINETEEN

CHARLIE DIAMOND'S JEWELLERY SHOP LOOKED DARK AND THE door was locked. Jade tapped on the glass. A buzzer sounded and the door clicked open by itself. Nervously, she stepped inside. She saw that it was full of dusty glass cases which contained jewellery. There were labels everywhere: Past-World, Antique, Gold, White Gold, Silver, Birthstones and many more. On the wall, behind the counter, were three clocks that all showed the same time. It was just past seventeen hours.

The shop was dim, with just some low lights dotted round the walls, but on the counter was a lamp that gave out a strong beam of light. A voice called out.

'What can I do for you?'

She peered into the dim interior.

'I'm looking for Charlie.'

'And who might you be?'

Charlie Diamond was behind the counter, sitting in an armchair. He angled the lamp so that she could see him. He was wearing circular glasses that had slid down his nose, and in one hand he had a huge magnifying glass. His white hair hung down each side of his face.

'I'm ... I'm Jade ... Big Frank's granddaughter. He wanted me to pick something up. I have a key,' she said, holding up the broken chain so that Charlie could see the key hanging neatly from it.

Charlie stood up, setting aside what he had been working on. His face looked grave and he shook his head. He took the chain and key from her hand.

'Does this mean what I think it does?'

Jade felt a lump in her throat.

'Granddaddy died yesterday. He was sick for a long time. I knew it was coming but it was hard to see him ...'

She welled up with tears. Using the back of her hand, she wiped them away. Charlie began to tut several times.

'I'm so sorry ... I knew he was ill ... Come around the counter. Sit here, in my chair. I will get you some tea.'

'No, I don't want ... I'm just here to get ...'

'We can talk about that in a moment. Hot sweet tea is

what's needed.'

He took Jade's arm and led her round the counter to the armchair and she sat in it. He turned the lamp off and the shop dimmed; only the wall lamps gave out a soft light.

Charlie opened a creaking door at the back of the shop and went through and she was left on her own. She closed her eyes and tried to calm herself. Now that she had her possessions back, she should have been relieved but there was still so much to do. Coming up against the warden had shaken her. She felt anxious; she couldn't help it.

She opened her eyes and glanced over at the door and was startled for a moment because there was a face at the glass. She leaned forward to get a better look but it vanished and, for a few seconds, she wondered if she'd imagined it. Someone *had* been looking though, she was sure, just as she had done earlier. That person was wearing a baseball cap, like the one that Bates wore.

A creak sounded and Charlie came back into the shop, holding a mug with steam coming out of it.

'Tea.'

She took the handle and drank from the cup. It was scalding hot and she felt it sliding down her throat.

'You drink this and I'll go and get your granddaddy's safe.'

Charlie went upstairs. She heard his footsteps above her and doors creaking open and shutting. Minutes later, he appeared carrying a small grey metal box. He placed it on the counter.

'Now, Jade. You need to open this.'

Charlie handed her the key.

Jade slid the key into the lock and turned it. Inside was a small black silk pouch with a drawstring. She picked it up and pulled it open, upending it so that four heavy coins fell out. They lay on the counter and Jade felt a moment's disappointment. What had she been expecting? Gold? Jewels? They looked, at first glance, like many of the coins that her granddaddy had scavenged from the sea.

She looked towards Charlie for some explanation.

'These are very precious, worth a lot of dollars,' he said, picking one up and showing it to her.

It was just a coin, a little larger than many she had seen and maybe a little thicker. Coins from past-world were popular; Granddaddy never had any trouble selling them.

'This is a sovereign,' he said. 'Sovereigns are made of gold but that's not the real reason why these four in particular are so valuable.'

Jade picked one up.

'Look at the date on it.'

It was hard to read but she held it up under the lamp on the counter.

'2042,' she said.

'That's it, 2042. The last year that sovereigns were minted.'

'Because of the Great Flood,' she said.

'You can see,' Charlie said, 'that the coin is engraved with an image of King William V. The last king before the flood. These coins are more valuable than any other sovereigns because there weren't many of them minted and they came from that terrible year.'

'They're worth *lots* of dollars?'

'Yes.'

'Why didn't granddaddy just sell them?'

She thought of his illness and not being able to afford meds or a visit to a clinic. And the way they lived in the Wetlands; sometimes there hadn't been enough food to eat or enough oil to light the lamps in their cabin. They'd shivered together during the ice-winter because they hadn't been able to buy fuel.

'We could have used the dollars,' she said, sadly.

'He knew that *and* he could have sold these ten times over. I know at least three buyers who would have come to an auction for them. No, no, no. He didn't want that. He kept them for you. That's why he gave them to me to look after. So that they'd be in a locked safe, here in my shop. That way, he knew he wouldn't be tempted to sell them. He wanted you to have them after he'd gone. So that you could afford to live well.'

'But . . .'

'Things have changed though, and now they must help

you get your sister back.'

She stared at him.

'How did you know about Mona?'

'Spike Raven, the ryder, brought me a letter from your granddaddy, just over two weeks ago.'

Of course. Spike must have called in to see Charlie after his last visit.

'Spike is the person who will sell these for you – for a high price. And he will help you get your sister back.'

'How will I find him?'

'All the ryders are in town now because of the rising water. They're at the Exchange every day at nine. It's where business is conducted.'

Jade stood up. She took the pouch with the coins and put it into her back-sack. She lifted it over one shoulder, ready to leave.

Charlie had opened a drawer at the counter and was rummaging about.

'Before you go, I have something you might like.'

He pulled out a past-world photograph and handed it to her. It was a picture of three young men. They were standing in a line, each with an arm around the other. They were wearing cut-off trousers and plastix foot-sandals. They were smiling.

'That's your granddaddy, Billy Benson and me. It was taken forty years ago when we were all young fishermen.'

'Before the first flood.'

'That's right. The world was very different then. We were great friends. We met up again when we worked together, building the dyke here at North-Hampton. Then I was given the right to live here but your granddaddy and BB had to stay in the Wetlands.'

'Why weren't they allowed to stay?

'Ah . . .'

Charlie raised his hands and gestured round the shop. Jade saw one glass case after another crammed with jewels. There was hardly any space that wasn't filled with precious objects.

'My father owned this shop, before the Great Flood. I was brought up on these streets. When he died – just after the deluge – he left this shop to me. I was allowed to stay because of this. Your granddaddy and BB were working men. They had nothing, so they had to live in the Wetlands.'

Jade looked more closely at the photograph. The three men were standing on a jetty and, on the deck, in front of them was a fish. It was big, and glistened in the sun. The men were smiling widely, her granddaddy's eyes screwed up against the bright light and BB was smoking a cigarette.

'What happened to BB? We saw him a lot then he just didn't come to Peter's Town anymore.'

Charlie shrugged his shoulders.

'He just disappeared, last I heard. Your granddaddy

thought he might have drowned while he was diving. But no one has seen him for a long time.'

Jade put the photograph into her back-sack.

'Thank you, Charlie.'

'Look after yourself, my dear.'

She nodded and, holding the back-sack tight, she left the shop.

TWENTY

BACK AT THE ENCAMPMENT THE SMELLS OF COOKING WERE IN the air. Jade queued up for soup and bread. When she'd finished eating, she headed for the East Bay Camp where she'd left the others earlier.

Old Mary was kneeling over a bubbling pot. Rosa was shredding up herbs.

'Mary's making another coction,' she said.

'Oh,' Jade said, 'I have some of these left.'

She pulled out the bag with the remaining poppy-pills.

'Thank you. These will be so useful.'

She walked outside and saw Samson sitting on the ground some metres away. He was outside a circle of people who were around a fire. He looked thoughtful. Jade, making sure her back-sack was firmly on her shoulder, walked across and sat down next to him.

'Where's Bates?' she said.

'Don't know. He went off. Seemed like he was in a bit of a mood.'

'Really? That's not like him.'

'You don't know him. You think you do, but you don't.'

Samson sounded *angry*. She was taken aback by his tone. She didn't know him either. Every exchange had been testy and brusque, but it wasn't his fault that he was in the position he was in. And he had got her dollar belt and key and chain back.

'Have you got the meds yet?' she said, gently.

'Some of them. Others I'll get tomorrow. There's a couple of people I have to find.'

'Why do you need them? I thought you said that the only people in your camp are those who've no longer got the pox?'

'These aren't pills for the pox. There are no pills for that. It either kills you or it doesn't. No, some of the Marines get ill from being old or they have a cancer. Sometimes they break a bone or become wounded. I get poppy-pills and other meds to stop infection.'

'How many people live on the boats . . .'

'Eighty-three, at the last count. A couple of people are very old but there's a mix of ages. There's about twenty kids under sixteen.'

Twenty kids. About as many as lived in Peter's Town.

She looked at the fire, the flames curling into the air, tiny sparks coming off the wood. Someone was singing nearby and others were joining in. Samson was quiet, his forehead in a frown. Jade's granddaddy's shirt was done tightly up to his neck and the sleeves hung over his knuckles. No one could tell he was a feral, but he wasn't one of *them.* It didn't matter that his face was the same, *he* was different.

'Where do you come from?' she said.

He frowned at her.

'I mean before you were ill. Where did you live?'

'High-Town.'

She was surprised. She had never met or spoken to anyone who had lived in High-Town. She certainly had no idea that people in High-Town got ill.

'When did you get . . . you know . . . the pox?'

'A couple of years ago. Maybe nearly three years ago. When I was ten or so.'

'Don't they have doctors there?'

'Smallpox is an epidemic. It doesn't matter where you live, if you come into contact with someone who has it and you're unlucky . . .'

'But you had to leave? What about your family?'

'You ask too many questions,' he said, looking pained.

'Sorry . . .'

Samson heaved a great sigh.

'I lived with my father and my sister. When I got ill, they had no choice but to let me go. So, me and about thirty other people – some old, some young – were expelled.'

'Oh.'

'It was a bad time, but we met others . . .'

'Other ferals?'

'We don't call ourselves *ferals*!'

'What, then?'

'We're just people. If you want to call us anything, then call us Wetlanders. It's where we live. It's how we live – off the water.'

'Do you miss the life you had?'

''Course I do. Every day, I think about my sister and my father.'

She chewed on her lip. She knew how that felt. She knew what it was to miss people. The singing got louder then, two or three people standing up linking arms.

Jade and Samson sat very still, their faces long, amid all the jollity.

TWENTY-ONE

JADE FOUND HERSELF A SPACE TO SLEEP JUST AS BATES CAME into the tent.

'Something wrong?' she said. 'Samson said . . .'

His face was closed.

'What is it?'

'I don't really know how to explain . . .' he said.

She waited. He took his cap off and punched at the middle of it. Then he put it back on again.

'The fisherman I lived with. He used to be Frank's partner.'

'Granddaddy's diving partner? BB? Why didn't you say something? Granddaddy would have loved to know what happened to BB!'

Jade remembered her granddaddy talking about his partner. They'd been diving together for years, but then BB got restless and wanted to dive further along the coast. Her granddaddy had to stay in Peter's Town because of Mona and Jade. He'd expected his partner to come back, but he hadn't.

'Billy told me some stuff before he died.'

Jade frowned. She thought of all the times she'd come back to the cabin and found Bates sitting with her granddaddy, listening to his stories. And yet, he hadn't once mentioned that he knew BB.

'Why didn't you say you knew him?'

Bates shrugged. Maybe he'd been grieving. She remembered that it had been hard to get more than a few words out of him at one time.

'Billy asked me to find Frank. He was angry with him.'

'Why?'

She felt her shoulders stiffen.

'He told me that he and Frank always shared unusual finds. Didn't matter which of them found it, they agreed they would always share the proceeds. He heard that Frank had found some valuable coins and he never got his share. He knew that the coins would be at the jeweller's shop in North-Hampton.'

She didn't answer. It was so *unexpected*. She remembered the face she had seen at the door of the shop. Had that person been Bates? Had he followed her there? She tucked her back-sack into her side.

'You came to Peter's Town,' she said, 'to find my granddaddy, because of the coins?'

'At first I did . . .'

Some children burst into the tent, chasing each other, laughing, shouting. The homers around shushed them.

'That's why you hung around, pretended to like him?'

'I *did* like him. He reminded me of Billy.'

'You talked to him, you were nice to him, but all the time it was because of these *coins*?'

She lowered her voice.

'It's hard to explain. Billy just wanted what was rightfully his. He asked me to do it and I felt I had to.'

'You waited for me while I was looking after Granddaddy. I thought you were a friend. And all the time you were there for something else.'

Bates pulled his cap lower over his eyes.

'Why didn't you just ask Granddaddy? If they had that agreement, he would have told you. That's the kind of man he was. He was fair.'

'He didn't come and find Billy though, did he? When he found the coins?'

Other people in the tent were looking at them.

'He did try!' she said in a loud whisper. 'He asked everyone who came to the village. No one knew where BB was. Then he became ill! By the time you arrived, he could barely walk to the end of the garden. You saw him!'

'Billy was right, though. Big Frank *had* left something with the jeweller.'

Jade looked down at her back-sack.

'So, what are you saying? You want BB's half? Is that it?'

'Yes . . . No . . . I mean, I did, before I came . . .'

'You can't have it!' she said, fiercely, thinking of Mona. 'I need it. And any way, you could be making this whole story up. Why should I trust you? After you lied to my granddaddy? Why should I?'

Bates's face tensed up.

'I never lied. I just didn't say.'

'It amounts to the same thing. You kept something important from him!'

'Like he kept something important from Billy!'

She stared at him. He looked different, as if she'd never really known him.

'I don't even want it anymore,' he said. 'Just wanted you to know that half of it was Billy's.'

He walked off, out of the tent. Jade felt her jaw trembling as if she was on the brink of tears. She would not cry though – not over some lying kid. In her bag, she had the coins and, tomorrow, there was an important job to do. She had no time or energy to think about a stupid boy.

TWENTY-TWO

SHE WOKE UP TOO EARLY. HER HEAD FELT HEAVY, AS IF SHE hadn't slept at all. There was noise and movement all around her. Rain was thudding on the roof of the tent and people were shouting. She sat up and saw people passing her towards the tent flap; going out, coming back in, calling to others, their faces full of panic.

'What's happening?' she called.

'It's dawn. The high tide is here. The water's up to the dyke!'

She didn't know who was speaking; the voice was lost among many others. Although she could see that it was just light outside, it seemed that everyone was instantly awake, getting to their feet, a look of fear on their faces.

Conversations were going on around her. She could also hear the water. The waves were pounding against the dyke, like a distant drum.

'Is it the high tide?'

'Is it the water?'

'How high is it?'

'Will the dykes hold?'

'We'll all be drowned.'

She got to her feet and grabbed her back-sack. People were moving around, picking up belongings, grabbing hold of children. She couldn't see Rosa or Old Mary. Samson came into the tent. He strode towards her.

'People are moving to higher ground, in case the dyke gives way.'

'Will it?'

'I don't think so. The wardens look calm. But people are panicking.'

'Where's Bates?' she said, remembering the horrible argument they'd had.

'He's gone.'

'Gone where?'

Jade moved out of the way to let some homers pass her. A small child was screaming with fright. The sound seemed to pierce through her eardrums. Just then, a wave must have hit the dyke full on; she could feel the vibrations coming from the ground beneath them.

'There's water!' someone shouted.

There was no water, Jade was sure, but she could smell the sea and feel its force. Samson was taking her arm, drawing her out of the tent. Outside, people were massing in a great crowd. Up in front there was a line of wardens. The rain was heavy, the sky grey. She could see the wardens talking to the homers, their hands gesturing in a calming way. The water was crashing against the dyke. Outside, it didn't sound so bad, more distant. She looked at the giant walls. They were bone dry, solid and hard. After a few moments, the homers had stopped shouting. She could see Rosa and Old Mary across the way. They must have been ministering to the sick. The homers settled, some of them joking with the wardens. Nervous laughter rippled across the crowd and people turned back towards the tents.

The waves continued to break against the walls.

'Bates said he wanted to start fresh . . .' Samson said.

'What?'

'He says it would be better if he went.'

'No!' she said. 'No, he can't go.'

'He has. He took his stuff late last night. He said you called him a liar.'

'Because he said things about my granddaddy. About . . .'

'I know about the coins. Bates thinks differently.'

'You don't understand. Even if I wanted to, I couldn't share them with him. I need them for an important reason . . .'

'None of my business. It's between you and Bates.'

Jade looked at Samson. There was something smug about him. When it came to Bates, he seemed to know much more than she did. She didn't say another word, but walked off out of the tent.

TWENTY-THREE

JADE SEARCHED FOR BATES. SHE STRODE THROUGH THE encampment, visiting homers from other villages, asking about a boy who wore a peaked cap. Many were sitting outside round campfires; having breakfast, washing their children, getting ready for the day. Just after seven hours, she saw Samson by the food tent. She walked over, her shoulders low.

'There's no sign of him. I don't know where else to look,' she said.

'In the town?'

'Would he go there?'

'He might. I'll come and help if you like . . .'

They walked down narrow streets and alleyways. Mostly Samson was a few feet ahead of her. There was no sign of Bates. They looked in shops and cafés. They asked some Wetlanders who were in the town. No one had seen him. They retraced their steps down the main thoroughfare.

She looked at Samson and felt a spurt of gratitude. He hadn't needed to come with her. It was dangerous for him to be so visible and yet, here he was, helping her. She thought about the things she'd said to him the night before.

'Do you think you'll ever see your family again?'

She quickened her steps to keep up with him.

'Might things change? Might you be allowed to go home?' she said, gently.

He glanced back. 'It's unlikely.'

His back was squared against her. She thought if she put her hand out to touch his shoulder, it would be hard and tight like a knotted rope.

'I'm sorry for you,' she said. 'That you lost your family. I never really thought about what happened to fer— people like you, who had the disease.'

'I know,' he said.

She touched him on the arm.

'I mean it. I was wrong. You, me and Bates, we've all lost our families.'

He nodded his head and she felt a lump in her throat. They were just three orphans, chasing around. She wished she could see Bates and explain to *him* why she'd been angry. The row had left a horrible feeling inside her. She'd thought of her granddaddy searching for Mona, travelling everywhere, day and night to find her. He hadn't done that for BB. BB hadn't been his kin but they'd been best friends for over forty years. She remembered him and BB in the past-world photograph that Charlie Diamond had given her. Friendship was important, wasn't it?

Had Bates been just a *little bit* right? She remembered when he brought the wheeling chair to the house, offering to help push Granddaddy all the way to North-Hampton. She'd thought him a good person then; she was sure she hadn't been wrong.

She kept staring into groups of people who passed by or were standing around, her eyes jumping from face to face, searching for him. There was a buzz of conversation in the air, people relieved that the high tide hadn't come into the town. She noticed a couple of wardens stopping to share a word with the residents of North-Hampton. One of them was the woman with the eye-glasses who had stopped Jade the evening before. She turned in their direction. She wasn't looking at Jade though. It was Samson she had focused on. A couple of the North-Hampton people stared as well and one of them said something to the other and he laughed.

They stood out. They were Wetlanders. Everything about them was different to the residents of the town. They looked scruffy, unhealthy probably. None of these people had any idea what sort of lives they lived. It made everything feel hopeless for a moment.

And she still had to go and see Spike at nine hours at the Exchange.

'Let's get out of here,' she said. 'There's somewhere we can go where no one will be watching us.'

Jade walked off towards the alleyways. Samson followed her as she headed for the steps her granddaddy had shown her a couple of years before. The area became rougher as she got closer. There were painted words on walls, words her granddaddy wouldn't have liked her to use. Turning off an alley, she went through an open area where bags of plastix sat, in piles, black and sweaty. The smell was very strong and Samson screwed his face up. A narrow path led away towards the dyke and half-way along it there was a clump of bushes and a dead tree, its branches bare and stiff. She pulled a large branch back and squeezed through. Samson followed and there were the spiral stairs. They opened a gate and walked through.

They were at the Crow's Nest.

'Wow . . .' Samson said.

Jade looked over the edge of the dyke to the Wetlands beyond. The sea had covered the land. It stretched from the horizon, all the way up to the slope on which the dyke was built. Thirty kilometres of water between here and Peter's

Town. In the middle, it was a solid mass, like quivering jelly, but at the edges it was foamy, sloshing against the rocky incline. It was too far below for her to feel any spray. There was a breeze that niggled at her neck; salt was in the air and she even fancied she could taste the grit of sand in her mouth. She thought of her village, which was underwater – the Worship-Hall on the sea bed, the play-park immersed, the swings being pushed and pulled by underwater tides. She pictured her books carried off the windowsill by the water, ruined, their stories lost forever.

'Where does all this water come from!' she said.

She didn't mean it as a question and Samson didn't answer because everyone knew where the water came from. They'd learned it in school lessons and from the older people in the Wetlands. Some of the ice at the north and south of the planet had melted and the sea level had risen. The seas had once been a benefit for people, allowing them to fish and travel and make energy from the waves. Now it had turned into an unpredictable enemy, making the weather too hot or too cold, throwing storms and angry winds toward the land. And, when it didn't seem as though things could get worse, it swelled up and swallowed their homes.

Samson had stopped looking at the sea. He was on the opposite side of the platform, looking across the roofs of North-Hampton. She stood alongside him.

'When did everything get so hard . . .' she said.

Samson looked at her.

'Hard for you but worse for us.'

'I know,' she said, 'I'm sorry for you and your people.' She gave a little smile.

'Except for the two robbers who stole from me . . . I can see why Bates felt comfortable with you.'

'When Bates came and lived with us, he was an angry boy,' Samson said. 'Always talking about Big Frank and how he would get the sovereigns that rightly belonged to Billy. I tried to keep him in Little-Venice for as long as I could so that he would heal a bit.'

Jade was chewed her lip.

'When I saw him yesterday, he was a different person. He was relaxed and friendly. None of the moods and outbursts that he'd had before.'

'He'd changed?'

'Yes. He's still as thin, and won't stop wearing that stupid cap, but he had none of the rage left.'

'How come?'

'He told me that he came to Peter's Town looking for the coins but instead he found a family.'

'Oh.'

'That's why he told you about Billy. He wanted to be honest. He doesn't care about the coins anymore.'

She didn't know what to say. Bates found a *family*. Her family.

TWENTY-FOUR

THE EXCHANGE WAS BUSY AT NINE HOURS BUT JADE SAW SPIKE straight away. He was taller than most of the other ryders and was standing astride his bi-cycle. There was a crowd of other ryders in the square. They all wore the orange bibs and had their bi-cycles nearby, festooned with bags and sacks and pouches, the handlebars hanging with chains and locks that they used to keep them from being taken away.

Bi-cycles were valuable miscellanies. Her granddaddy always sold the ones he found straight away. Jade remembered the way he restored them. *We'll bring them back from their watery grave and breathe new life into them.* It took days, sometimes weeks, of work to get a bi-cycle working well. Then he would take it up to North-Hampton and sell to the highest bidder. Often, he brought bits of bikes with him – wheel arches, handlebars, seats – and got rid of those too.

Spike looked up and saw her. He raised a hand and beckoned her to come over. She felt instantly shy. He was an imposing figure, not just because of his height but his hair was different: most of it plaited into long braids and stiffened as though he'd coated it with mud. In Peter's Town she'd always gotten out of the way when Spike came around, although Mona had loved to chat to him about the things he saw on his travels around the Uplands. He always shook Jade's hand rigorously and called her *kid*, which she had liked at first but later felt embarrassed about. He usually had some time to sit on the porch and talk to her granddaddy, and Mona was always there as well. It made Jade slink away, not being able to get a word in the conversation.

'Hi,' she said. 'Charlie Diamond said to come and see you ...'

'I was really hoping you would come. Big Frank?'

'He died, the day before yesterday.'

'I'm so sorry, kid. He was a lovely guy. He's not the first diver I heard about who died like that. There were chemicals under the water, all the around the wrecks he dived into. He knew there was a risk.'

Jade had always thought that her granddaddy had

swallowed the chemicals by accident, not that he'd *known* they were there and dived into them anyway.

'He had to earn a living like the rest of us,' Spike said.

She didn't know what to say.

'Why don't we go somewhere a bit more private so we can talk?' he said.

He manoeuvred his way towards a covered area alongside a tavern. As he went, some of the other ryders looked round and patted him on the shoulder. Everybody seemed to know him, even the prentices. Jade was surprised to see some female ryders there. Spike leaned his bi-cycle up against the wall and sat on a bench. She sat alongside him.

'You see this bi-cycle?'

Jade had seen it many times.

'Your granddaddy got it for me. Three years ago. I'd been a prentice for a long time and wanted to get a licence to go into the Uplands. There were only a few licences for sale. I had the money to pay for it but it meant I didn't have enough left to buy any wheels. I asked him if he'd let me pay it off and he said he would. No one else would have done that; he trusted me for the dollars.'

It sounded true. It was the odd sort of thing her granddaddy would have done. She wished that Bates was sitting next to her so he could hear this good report.

'I paid him back, 'course I did. That's why I used to come around a lot. And I liked Mona too. She was such a bright kid. I thought she could be a prentice. I told Frank I'd teach her. I couldn't understand why she went off. And then when I saw her . . .'

'How was it that you saw her? '

'I was delivering a package to the Butterfly Palace and I noticed this scrawny-looking girl. She was sitting in a window seat. It took a few moments before I realised it was her. She couldn't see me but I know the domestic there and she told me about her circumstances.'

'Why is she even there?'

'The man who runs the place – his name is the Duke – he *owns* her.'

'What?'

'I don't think Mona ever found any secure work. She pawned her belongings and then she borrowed money from a dollar-shark. They were threatening to have her arrested and sent to Landfill but the Duke stepped in. He paid her debts so she has to work for him to pay it off.'

'That's not right!'

He nodded, his eyes suddenly sharp and angry.

'You have the sovereigns?'

She pulled the pouch out of her back-sack and gave it to him.

'You'll pay her debt off with these?' Jade said.

Spike smiled but shook his head.

'She's been there for four months. Four months ago, these

sovereigns might have bought her out. But every week that goes by means that the amount she owes increases. So now it would cost ten times more to buy her out than it would have done at the beginning. Men like the Duke often buy people's debts. It means that young people in these situations end up working for them forever. The authorities don't care. It keeps them off the streets so they turn a blind eye.'

'Oh.'

'*And* the Duke's brother is a High-Warden.'

'What can you do?'

'I have some ideas and contacts in High-Town. First, I have arrangements to make and I have these to sell.'

He held the bag up in the air and let the sovereigns rattle together.

'I want you to come back here at about fifteen hours. We will go into High-Town tonight and get Mona out.'

'How?' she said, with some alarm.

'I'll tell you the details later. You will need a friend to help you. Someone who will hide Mona away from the authorities.'

Jade thought of Samson. And Bates, if he was still around somewhere.

'Don't worry, it will work out. You can hide Mona until the tide begins to recede. Then the whole of North-Hampton will be in chaos as they'll be desperate to get the Wetlanders out. Mona will be able to leave without anyone knowing.'

He was looking straight at her.

'Does that sound OK?'

'Yes.'

'Let's shake on it, kid!'

She put her hand out and he shook it firmly, making her arm move up and down as if he was pumping it. Then he got his bi-cycle and wheeled it away.

She sat still, twisting her fingers round each other. Mona had never found work. When Old Mary saw her in Little-Norfolk, she had been sitting by herself on the edge of the market. Perhaps she had been desperate and had no one to turn to. It made Jade feel wretched to think of it. There had been times, after Mona had left, especially when her granddaddy first got ill, that she'd thought of Mona with anger. Mona had escaped their life. Mona was living on a farm somewhere, making a lot of dollars, and had forgotten about them. Maybe she was using the dollars to buy sparkles and flimsies and trips to see the minstrels.

But Mona wasn't comfortable. She wasn't with the minstrels.

She was stuck in the house of a man who *bought* people.

TWENTY-FIVE

JADE COULD SEE SAMSON SITTING OUTSIDE THE TENT WITH OLD Mary and Rosa. He was tearing off strips of bandage, handing them to Rosa who was rolling them up. Old Mary was grinding something on a stone that looked dark and unpleasant.

Some small boys and girls were playing. They were passing a ball by hand and trying to bounce it into a chalk circle. There was shouting and laughing and red faces. Jade watched them with envy. They were carefree. She hadn't felt like that for a long time.

She was apprehensive about the job she had to do. A lot depended on it.

What if it all went wrong?

She heard a voice from behind.

'Jade.'

It was Bates. He walked up alongside her. She smiled widely.

'I'm sorry . . .' he said.

She wanted to put her arm around him, to give him a hug, but he would have been too embarrassed. Instead, she kept talking.

'No, it's me who should be sorry. I was in the wrong . . . I was totally to blame . . . I shouldn't have called you a liar'

'I could have told Frank . . .'

Samson was walking towards them. He gave Bates a slap on the back. How easy it was for boys to show their feelings. All she had was words.

'I can explain about the coins,' she said.

Bates dismissed her comment with a wave of his hand, as if to say *I don't care.*

'I'm too hungry,' he said. 'I need some food.'

'Let's go and see if there's any sugar-rolls at the food-hall,' Samson said.

'No, really, this is important. There's something I haven't told you. Granddaddy asked me to keep it a secret. But now I need to explain because I need help from both of you.'

'I need to eat. You can tell us on the way,' Bates said, pushing his cap up so that she could see his eyes.

'It's about my sister Mona . . . She's in trouble . . . That's why I couldn't give you half . . .'

The food-hall was quiet and they sat at the first table they came to. Samson got the cakes and they ate hungrily. The sugar-rolls were sticky and Jade had to keep licking her fingers. The cup of tea was hot enough to burn the roof of her mouth. Bates was looking happier. Samson was wiping the sugar from the corner of his mouth with the sleeve of granddaddy's shirt.

'I've seen this ryder, Spike,' Samson said, 'but I haven't done any business with him. Are you sure he's someone you can trust?'

'He was a friend of my granddaddy.'

'But your granddaddy's gone now. You have to be careful.'

She thought about it for a moment.

'Granddaddy depended on him. That's good enough for me.'

Samson shrugged. He seemed to be thinking hard.

'Where exactly is your sister?' he said.

'In a place called the Butterfly Palace.'

'I know it. It's a couple of streets from where I lived. It's run by the Duke. Not a nice place.'

'Who is the *Duke*?' Bates said.

It was something she'd been thinking about ever since she'd left Spike.

'He's the brother of one of the High-Wardens. He's supposed to be respectable but everyone knows he isn't.

The Butterfly Palace is a club, but lots of bad things happen there and the Garda – the men who patrol the town – turn a blind eye.'

'Mona is there and she's not free to leave.'

'Oh.'

She explained about the Duke "owning" Mona.

'That's why I need you. I've got to rescue her. If it works out, she'll need to hide here until we can leave North-Hampton. Will you help?'

"Course,' Bates said.

'No problem,' Samson said.

TWENTY-SIX

AT FIFTEEN HOURS, SHE WAS SITTING ON THE SAME BENCH where she and Spike had talked that morning. There were some ryders around, playing hand-cards on the ground. Wardens were walking up and down, talking to passing townspeople. One or two of them glanced disapprovingly at her.

It seemed a long time until Spike came into the square. He was riding an engine-bike that she hadn't seen him use before. The bike buzzed along, the noise making everyone turn round. Most people looked away immediately, uninterested, but the wardens watched as the engine-bike pulled up a few steps away from Jade.

Spike got off.

'We'll go soon. Can you look after this racer for me? I just have to get something from a friend and we'll be on our way.'

She watched him walk up to one of the wardens. The man laughed as if he'd just heard the funniest joke. Everyone liked Spike. Good ryders had to be like that, her granddaddy had told her. They were scruffy or even quite weird-looking but that was OK because they were useful. They did deals with all sorts of people and couldn't afford to have any enemies. Once they'd got their licences, ryders were allowed to go anywhere. They did business all over the Wetlands, the towns and the Uplands. They were trusted because their licences were hard to get. A new ryder had to be a prentice for a certain amount of time and then wait until a space became available.

Spike went into the tavern.

She stood by the racer, feeling the heat coming from the engine. It was chunkier than a bi-cycle and it had two seats. Jade had seen a couple out in the wetlands, mostly from a distance; the ryder in the front seat and the passenger clinging on. Her granddaddy had marvelled at these vehicles. He'd said that as a young man he'd had one and driven around in it. It had been his wish to fish one out of the water but he'd never done it.

She looked at her timer. It was a little past fifteen hours.

Was there time to get into High-Town, find Mona *and* get out again?

'Jade.'

She heard her name being spoken and turned to see that Samson was standing there. She was surprised. He was holding Bates's cap.

'Bates is helping Rosa. He asked me to give you this. It's a good way of hiding who you are.'

'Thanks.'

'The other thing is,' Samson said, 'I want to ask you a favour but if you can't do it, it doesn't matter . . . I'll understand. No problem.'

He pulled a piece of paper out of his pocket and handed it to her. On it was a rough hand-drawn map. She could see the Butterfly Palace at the corner but streets were drawn beside it and on one of them there was an X. Beside it was a name and address:

Mr Philip Hall, 10 Marshall Street.

'It's where my father and sister live.' He lowered his voice. 'If you get time – and if you don't that's all right – go to my old house and tell them that I'm alive and that I'm all right and that I think about them every day. They call me *Samuel*.'

She stared at the map and didn't know what to say. She already had this heavy responsibility of trying to get her sister out of High-Town. Could she do this as well? She folded the paper over and over and put it into her pocket.

'If you can't, that's OK,' Samson said.

Spike's voice called out from across the square. She saw Samson staring at him. His looks seemed outlandish and she could see why anybody would be uneasy.

'This is Samson,' she said, when Spike got to them. 'He and my other friend Bates are helping me with Mona.'

Spike grabbed Samson's hand and shook it heartily. He turned to Jade.

'We'll get going,' he said, taking hold of the engine bike. 'You need to get changed. I'll be over by the tavern.'

Samson stood close to her, his voice lower.

'I know you said you trust him but take care. It's not like you know much about him.'

'I'll be careful.'

'Good luck,' he said.

She watched him go.

I didn't know much about you until yesterday, she thought. And yet, now she felt like she would trust Samson with anything. That's why Bates thought of him as a close friend. She put her hand in her pocket and touched the piece of paper that he'd given her. Then she headed towards the tavern and Spike.

TWENTY-SEVEN

THEY LEFT NORTH-HAMPTON. THE RACER ROARED BENEATH HER and she clung on to Spike's waist, feeling as though she was hanging on to some flying creature. She was wearing a prentice's orange bib and it was fastened tightly so there was no chance of it coming off.

They were going up a long slope that seemed to go on forever, even though High-Town was only two kilometres ahead. She glanced back and saw North-Hampton getting further away; the turnstiles that they'd come through looked tiny.

Up ahead, the road widened out and there was a queue of vehicles. Jade had never seen so many in one place: lorries, trucks, red-buses, passenger-cars and motor-trikes. Spike slowed the racer down and at times had to put one foot on the ground to keep it balanced. They came up behind a truck that had wooden crates in the back, as well as a goat. Alongside them were some ryders; one of them leaned across and gave Spike a playful shove.

Jade could smell the petrol, like the chemicals from the estuary, where she and Bates had been a couple of days before. The oily stink seemed to hang in the air, making it feel heavy and warm, and the prentice bib felt tight around her chest.

It gave her a bad feeling.

When she was younger her granddaddy had told her that it was the petrol and the fuels that caused the floods to happen. It was a day when Mona had been in a world of her own, dressing up, playing a game with some cloth dolls she had. Jade had been interested though. *How come?* she'd said. Her granddaddy was cleaning his diving-fins. The fins sat on the grass, three pairs, the newest ones made of light plastix, bought from a ryder in North-Hampton. *Well,* he'd said, *people just pulled the fuels from deep in the ground and used them for everything. They gave power to machines, every kind. You could have a toothbrush that cleaned your teeth quickly or an aeroplane that flew across the sky to another country.* Jade had watched her granddaddy wash the fins with soapy water, his fingers probing the folds with suds. *You could fly like a bird,* he was saying. She wasn't thinking about the flying bit though, she was picturing the toothbrush that buzzed around the mouth. All she had was a brush with flattened tufts that she poked around her teeth. *Anyway,* he'd said, his voice cutting into her thoughts, *all those machines made the earth heat up and melted the ice at the poles. The weather changed but people took no notice. They continued to build more machines and use more fuel. Then the Great Flood came.*

Mona had started singing then, a song about a girl who was in love with a prince, and granddaddy looked proudly over at her. *She has a lovely voice,* he said, forgetting about the toothbrush and the other machines. Granddaddy loved Mona the best, Jade had always known that.

Now, the smell of the petrol seemed to have boxed her in. Spike didn't notice it. She tried to hold her breath. They began to move ahead and a slight breeze cleared the air.

She could see the distinct shape of a town. She expected High-Town to be huge, the biggest place on earth. People spoke about it with awe and their voices were hushed. It was also referred to with fear – the place where decisions were made by the High-Wardens and punishments were handed out.

She imagined tall buildings, maybe even some moving staircases. There were railway-trains, people had said, and many shops. Everyone in High-Town had pockets full of dollars. It would be clean and smooth as well, with no bad smells and people there would always look as though they had just stepped out of a bath.

But she found herself frowning the closer they edged towards it.

It was small. It was old.

After a short while, some wardens walked among the vehicles and siphoned them into different lanes. Spike, as well as other ryders, headed towards the lower walls of the town. They joined a queue which moved forward more quickly. The wall of the town was broken up by ornate metal gates. Jade sat up as high as she could to see the buildings beyond, but her view was barred by trees. The entry points were dotted with men in dark-green uniforms holding long-guns: the Garda.

The racer moved forward and then Spike stopped it and swung his leg over and stepped off. He held it steady so that she could do the same. He was careful with her, making sure she didn't lose her balance. She remembered then what Samson had said: *Be careful.* Her granddaddy had trusted Spike, although it was true that *she* didn't know anything much about him.

'I was wondering,' she said, after a few moments, 'how did you know granddaddy?'

'I was his ryder.'

'I know *that*, but how did you first meet him? He seems to have really liked you . . . like you're sort of family . . .'

She shrugged, embarrassed.

'You mean, how come he *trusted* me to help you?' Spike said, grinning.

'Not exactly . . .'

She looked away, her neck reddening. It was as if he knew what she was thinking.

The queue edged forward.

'I knew Frank from years ago. Me and my brother, Jase, we lived in an old industrial place on the North-Hampton road. There were a few others who lived there but mostly people kept themselves to themselves. I was only twelve then and my brother was four and I was looking after him. I used to carry him around on my back – like a piggy-back, you know?'

She nodded.

'We were going to the pontoon-market and Frank came along and walked with us and he said that soon my brother would be too big to carry. I must have been feeling in a black mood because I started to cry. I knew it was true – soon I wouldn't be able to carry him around. Frank kept saying sorry, that he was only joking, but then I put Jase down on the ground and Frank could see that his legs were wasted and that he couldn't walk. If I couldn't carry him then I didn't know what I was going to do.'

'Oh,' Jade said.

'Anyway, a few weeks later Frank comes to the place where

I lived and he's got this wheeling-chair with him. Brilliant, it was. He said he found it by the side of the road but it was too good for that. He said he thought of me and Jase and we could use it for as long as we wanted.'

Jade felt a lump in her throat.

'We used it for a couple of years. Until the ice-winter. Then Jase died and I took the wheeling-chair back to Peter's Town. I wheeled it all the way back to Frank. We put it in your church just in case anyone else ever needed it.'

The queue started to move and Spike put his finger over his lips to stop the conversation. Jade pictured the wheeling-chair sitting at the end of their garden. The brakes hadn't worked but they still might have been able to use it.

They were at the front of the queue and the Garda stepped towards them, his long-gun across his front, his face long, his mouth pinched.

'Packages to deliver . . .' Spike said.

The Garda coughed behind one of his hands. 'Anything for me?'

'Funny you should say that. I have one here.'

Spike pulled a tiny package from up his sleeve and put it into the hand of the Garda. The man looked from right to left and behind. Then he pocketed the package.

He nodded and Spike threw his leg over the racer. Jade did the same and the bike went through the iron gates and into High-Town. Even though the bike wasn't going fast, Jade held tightly to Spike. If it hadn't been so noisy, she would have told him about how Bates had found the wheeling-chair and how – for a few moments – it had seemed like they might be able to take her granddaddy with them to the dyke at North-Hampton.

TWENTY-EIGHT

THE FIRST THING JADE NOTICED ABOUT HIGH-TOWN WAS HOW quiet it was. As soon as they got through the gates there was a kind of hush. The noise of the queues and vehicles from outside seemed blocked off. They turned right and headed for a narrow lane that twisted and turned and wove down the side of a hill. They came to an archway and followed other vehicles underneath. The sky closed off and they were under a low roof that looked like it was made of corrugated iron, like the roof of the Worship-Hall in Peter's Town. There were gaps from time to time that let in strips of light. Spike pulled the racer into a space beside a line of other vehicles.

'This is where we park,' he said. 'Only red-buses allowed in High-Town.'

'Why?'

'High-Town people don't want to breathe in tainted air. The town is small – just two kilometres long and less than one wide.'

The air under the corrugated iron roof smelled worse than in the traffic queue.

'Come on, we don't want to spend too long in here.'

They walked out into the daylight and headed for a flight of steps that had been cut into the incline. Jade shifted and fidgeted with the orange bib she was wearing that had PRENTICE stamped across the shoulders. She took Bates's cap out of her bag and put it on, pulling the peak down over her forehead. She glanced inside at the package she was to give to the housekeeper.

'Let's go over the plan,' Spike said, slowing down. 'You're my prentice,' he said, 'so what do we do when we get there?'

'I go to the side entrance of the Butterfly Palace. I ring the bell and I hand the package to the housekeeper.'

'OK.'

'She will take the package and let me in and take me to Mona . . . will she?'

Jade faltered. Her confidence slipped. She looked round and registered that she really was in High-Town. *Illegally.* How could Spike be so sure that it would go smoothly?

'The housekeeper will be paid well. In the package is a wad of dollars. This is where most of the money from the sale of the sovereigns has gone.'

She pictured the sovereigns for a moment. Thick and gold, something beautiful that had been rescued from a sunken ship. Treasure. Now they had changed into dollars – paper money – and had been dispersed to a number of people.

'It'll be all right if you just play your part,' Spike said, patting her on the shoulder.

They walked through an opening and stepped into the streets of High-Town. Jade's mouth opened with surprise. She'd seen that the town was old but she hadn't expected the greenery. Everywhere that she looked there were trees and grass and borders of flowering hedges. She stood still for a moment, taking it all in. They were at the edge of a square that was paved and in the centre was a circular trough full of water which had a spout coming out of the side and spilled into another trough below it. Around it were several brown pots full of colourful flowers which wafted and rustled in the breeze.

'Come on!' Spike hissed. 'Try not to look too astonished by it all.'

She followed him across the square, glancing at groups of High-Town people who were sitting at café tables and drinking from china cups and saucers. They were smiling at each other and some were playing chess, moving their pieces with deliberation. A house-cat was sitting by someone's foot, its tail swishing. People were calm and it was so quiet she could hear her own footsteps. Looking closer though, she could see that pairs of Garda were dotted around, their hands resting on long-guns, their eyes piercing the square.

Two kilometres away, the sea was battering at the dykes of North-Hampton, but here it was like another world. She knew that if the dykes gave way then a different klaxon would sound, a signal for the townspeople of North-Hampton to get their belongings and get on the buses to come here. Then *they* would be living in tented camps until the threat was over.

Would the people of High-Town be quite so tranquil then? And what would happen to the Wetlanders?

They went down an alleyway and walked along by a small stream. Opposite were buildings with windows and balconies and she saw a domestic in a blue uniform standing, shaking out a piece of linen. Jade had one of those very uniforms in her back-sack. She found herself patting the bag nervously.

She noticed the bird cages then – dozens of them. They were different colours: black, yellow, green and silver. Inside were small brown birds. The cages sat on window ledges or dangled from brickwork. Spike must have seen her looking.

'This is called "Birdcage Alley". No surprise there.'

She was puzzled. How strange to keep birds in cages.

'Why . . .'

'Never mind. Keep focused. We'll be there in a minute.'

They stopped at the edge of another, larger square. There

were tall buildings all around, some more modern than she had seen previously. In the middle of the square, two trees were planted close together so that their branches made a kind of shelter from the sun. Underneath was a bench. Spike headed for the shaded area.

'These are called the *Saints*,' he said, patting the bark of one of them, 'They're oak and were planted many years before the Great Flood. They survived and are important to the people of High-Town.'

She looked at the trunk of the nearest tree. On it there was a plaque. She read the words:

IN REMEMBRANCE OF THE
GREAT FLOOD OF 2042

'THE DROWNING DAY'
MAY WE NEVER FORGET
THOSE THAT WE LOST

She frowned at the inscription. Something was missing.

'It doesn't mention the second flood.'

'The second flood didn't hit High-Town.'

'Oh.'

She looked around. Along one side of the square were two red-buses parked neatly, their doors wide open. Inside one, several people were sitting, still wearing their blue uniforms.

This was where the domestics came to get their buses back to North-Hampton.

Spike nudged her and pointed to a building on the far side of the square. It was at the edge of a row of tall houses and it was low, possibly only one level high. It had a wooden fence along the front and she could see foliage spilling over the sides, plants dangling to the ground, like ropes that could be climbed.

'That is the Butterfly Palace. The Duke is out for the afternoon.'

Her eye settled on the upper part of the building. It had a flat roof, where all those of the other buildings were steeped. Many of the homes in Peter's Town had flat roofs. They were easier to build but they often leaked water if there was heavy rainfall.

'That's where Mona is. Mrs Hendrix, the housekeeper, knows that you're coming. Remember, when she opens the door you have to say . . .'

'Package for Hendrix,' Jade said.

'Good. Not nervously but with gusto. As though you've done it lots of times before. You don't know who will be listening. Are you ready?'

She nodded.

'I'll wait here. Remember to explain everything to Mona so that we can get going quickly. It mustn't look as though she is nervous or out of place.'

'I will.'

'I'll be here, under the Saints, waiting for you.' He grabbed her hand and shook it gently. 'Go . . .'

Her heart pumping, she walked off across the square, towards the Butterfly Palace.

TWENTY-NINE

THE HOUSEKEEPER WAS STANDING WITH HER HANDS ON HER hips. She was a big lady, her blue uniform stretching tightly across her stomach. She was smiling with her mouth but the rest of her face was still.

'I've been expecting you.'

'Package for . . . for Hendrix . . . Hendrix,' Jade said, her words stuttering.

She held out the wrapped package. Her arm was trembling.

The housekeeper snatched it from her and stood back from the door. With one hand she tore open the brown paper. Inside was a bundle of dollars. Then she looked up and smiled widely.

Jade stepped inside. She could see other girls working; one was sweeping the floor, another was at the sink, a third was pummelling some dough on a worktop. They weren't wearing the blue uniform and she wondered if they too were *owned*.

'Follow me,' Mrs Hendrix said and strode through the kitchen, shooing the girls out of her way. 'She knows you're coming. I told her.'

Jade took Bates's cap off and went gingerly down a flight of stairs into a cellar. She didn't like places that were underground. In the Wetlands there was only water beneath the earth. Here, there was a damp smell and the walls seemed shiny with condensation. The passage was lit with a string of lights along the roof. She could see a door up ahead and Mrs Hendrix marched up to it and flung it open.

'She's over there. I know you got some changing of clothes to do. Don't take too long. The Duke is out at present and I don't *expect* him back, but he could turn up at any time.'

Jade walked further into the room. There were four beds and some screens that stood between them. She looked for Mona but couldn't see her. In the corner a child was sitting on a bed hugging her knees. She had long hair and appeared grubby. She looked at Jade but then buried her face in her knees.

Jade waited a second, thinking she had misunderstood the housekeeper and that her sister would come in, but no one came. She was exasperated. She would have to go back along the passage and get Mrs Hendrix. She turned to walk towards the door but stopped when she heard a tiny voice.

'Jade.'

She spun round. The child was saying her name. She stepped forward just as the girl got up off the bed and stared at her. She was slight and her cheekbones stuck out. Jade could see her twisting her fingers around each other as she spoke.

'It's me. It's Mona.'

'What?'

Jade couldn't say another word. Her eye travelled up and down this thin girl, her hair hanging in rat's tails, her clothes too big for her, her elbows sticking out.

'I know I've changed,' she said, in a soft voice that Jade could barely hear. 'I look different now. You must be shocked.'

'Mona?'

It wasn't the same person. Two years before, she had had to look *up* at her sister. She had been a little girl then but still, *this* Mona had shrunk.

'What's happened to you?'

The girl walked forward and flung her arms around Jade and clung tightly.

'Oh, Mona,' Jade said, her throat dry as paper.

'Where's granddaddy?' Mona said. 'Is he here? Is he outside?'

Jade bit her lip. She didn't know how to answer. She held Mona tightly to her chest. There was so much she had to tell her.

Later, when Mona had calmed down a little, the housekeeper came into the room.

'You need to get a move on,' she said. 'One of the other domestics said she saw the Duke nearby. He must have come back earlier than planned. I will let you out of the basement door. There are some steps leading up to the square. That way you won't run into him.'

'How will I know who he is? I've never seen him.'

'He's all in black and he wears a hat. He just looks different to anyone else. Mona will know him.'

'Thank you.'

The housekeeper looked at Mona.

'This is a good time to get her out. She's hardly said a word for weeks. She'll be sixteen soon and the Duke will use her in his club. That's if he hasn't already. It's the kind of work that I wouldn't want my daughter to do. He's a bad person.'

Jade didn't know what to say. She'd heard stories about girls who ended up being sold to different men.

Mona seemed to sink into herself. Jade grabbed her sister's hand.

'Mrs Hendrix, why do you work for him if he's such a bad man?'

'Dollars,' she said, without any hesitation. 'To feed my mother and my daughter. They come first for me. But if I can help someone else, I will try to do it.'

'For the dollars,' Jade said softly, remembering the small package she gave her.

'Yes, and I'm not ashamed of it. Now, don't take too long. I'll leave the door unlocked. The Duke doesn't need to know that she's gone missing until tomorrow morning. Then I'll tell him that she broke the lock on one of the windows and that she left to follow the minstrels. He knows that she likes them.'

She bustled off. Jade heard keys jangling and a lock being opened.

'Mona, we don't have much time.'

She reached into her back-sack and pulled out the blue uniform of a domestic.

'We need to get changed quickly and get out of here. Spike – you remember Spike? He's waiting outside.'

Mona stood silently but looked nervous.

'If the Duke finds out . . .'

'You have to do this. It was granddaddy's wish.'

'The Duke *owns* me.'

Jade felt her confidence slip. She tried to keep her face straight.

'Nobody *owns* anybody,' she said. 'We've got to get you out of here. Now.'

Mona looked unconvinced.

'Quickly, we have to get dressed.'

Jade started to take off the orange prentice bib. Mona put her hand on Jade's arm.

'I'm sorry, Jade. I messed it all up. I'm so sorry I ran away.'

'I know,' Jade said. 'I know you are.'

THIRTY

JADE WENT UP THE STEPS TO THE SQUARE. SHE HAD ON THE blue overall of a domestic worker over her clothes. Mona was close behind, wearing the prentice orange bib and Bates's cap. Jade glanced back at her. Mona wouldn't be recognised, she was sure. At the top Jade stopped and looked left and right and then around the space where the trees stood. She didn't know who she was looking for, other than a man in black with a hat.

'Can you see him?' she whispered to Mona.

Mona peered forward, her small face pale in the daylight. She shook her head.

'Come on.'

They walked towards the Saints. Mona seemed to straighten up and walk taller. The sun was low in the sky but the trees threw a circle of shadow on to the square and Jade was relieved to see Spike standing there waiting for them. When they got to him he held out his hand for Mona to shake.

'Very good to see you, my girl,' he said. 'I'm so sorry about your granddaddy. He and I were good friends.'

Mona gave a quivering smile. She kept looking back to the Butterfly Palace.

'The Duke's been seen, so the housekeeper said,' Jade said, her voice low.

'So, this is not the place to talk. We need to get on our way.'

'What if he comes? He'll see me!' Mona said.

'No, he'll see a ryder and his prentice. We will be OK.'

'You'll take her to the camp, to Samson and Bates?'

'And you, my girl, will get on the red-bus back to North-Hampton.'

'I will,' she said.

She wasn't intending to get the *first* bus back.

Spike and Mona walked off. Mona looked back every few steps but Jade waved her on. She watched them go towards Birdcage Alley. When they were out of sight she looked carefully round the square, searching for a man in a black outfit, but there was no one like that. A pair of Garda stood talking near one of the corners, but they soon moved off. She looked back towards the red-buses. A short line of male and female domestics were queuing to get on the first one. She had plenty of time because last bus went at twenty hours, Spike had told her.

She was able to relax for a few moments. She patted the pocket of the blue uniform and pulled out the piece of paper that she'd put there. Samson's map was simple and there was an arrow by the Butterfly Palace. She walked back towards it and saw that the street opposite was called Saints Parade. She had to walk down there and take the second turning on the right to get to Marshall Street.

Marshall Street was a narrow alley which widened out as it went along. There were shops selling foodstuffs. She paused at them, looking hungrily at the items in the window. Further along there was a row of houses and it wasn't long before she was standing in front of a door that had the number *10* on it. She tried to breathe evenly but felt her nerves tingling in her neck. Was she losing her courage? Turning her back on the house, she made herself look across the street. There was a small school play-park under the shade of some flowering trees. There were no children in it but there was a climbing frame made from metal struts. There had been a similar one in Peter's Town; it was not as big and didn't have tiny footholds in the sides, nor did it have soft flooring underneath in case any small child fell down. This one cost more dollars and was probably a lot more fun to play on. And yet she could remember when she was very young and Mona had thrust her up on to the top level so that she had to climb down all by herself. She'd been fearful then, but Mona had been there to stop her hurting herself. She wondered if Samson had ever held his sister up to this climbing frame and waited for her to work her way down.

She turned back to the house and knocked on the door. After a few moments it was opened by a man. He was holding a book and he had eye-glasses on.

'Yes?' he said, distractedly.

'Excuse me, are you Mr Hall?'

'Yes, yes . . .' he said, glancing up at her.

'I have a message . . .'

He looked her over and seemed to take in her uniform.

'It's not my day for cleaning. I told the agency—'

'I'm not here to clean. I have a message from . . . from your son.'

Mr Hall stared at her as if he hadn't quite heard. Then his face changed, he shut the book crisply and put it under his arm. He took his eye-glasses off and it was as if he was seeing her clearly for the first time.

'Who are you?' he said.

'I can't say and I don't have long, but your son, Samson – I mean, *Samuel* –asked me to come and see you.'

'Samuel?'

'Is Samuel's sister here? He said the message was for both of you.'

The sound of footsteps came along the alley and she glanced back. Two Garda were walking in her direction. She felt her face freeze. *She shouldn't have come. She should have gone straight to the bus.* Mr Hall must have registered her alarm because he reached out, grabbed her arm, and pulled her inside the hallway and shut the door behind her. They both stood still and listened until the footsteps of the Garda had passed by.

'Now . . .' he said.

'Samuel . . . I call him *Samson*, he told me to tell you and his sister that he is alive and all right and that he thinks about you every day.'

Mr Hall seemed stunned. He appeared to lose balance for a second and she put her hand out to steady him. He put his eye-glasses on but then took them straight off.

'Where is he?' he whispered.

'I can't tell you that.'

'Where does he live? How does he exist?'

'I can't say. And I have to go in a minute because I shouldn't be here in High-Town.'

'Wait, wait . . . can you give him something from me? Can you take something small?'

She nodded.

'Hang on . . .' He disappeared into the room and she heard

drawers opening and shutting and a low voice, as if he was talking to himself. She peeped inside. There was a screen and a couch and some medical equipment. She'd seen items like it in the Free-Clinic years before. Samson's father was a medic.

'I'll be with you in a second,' he called.

She remembered the Garda then and began to feel agitated. There was no reason for them to speak to her. Spike had told her that they patrolled but they rarely bothered with domestics. The only place that people were questioned or searched was when they were trying to get *into* High-Town. Once they were inside or were leaving, nobody much cared.

The door opened and Mr Hall came out. He had a small white envelope in his hand. The end was open but it looked as though there was paper stuffed into it.

'Can you give this to Samuel?'

She took it and folded it in half and put it into her back-sack.

'What's your name? I'd like to know.'

'Jade,' she said.

'Where are you from?'

'The Wetlands. We came to North-Hampton . . .'

'Because of the flood,' he said.

'Yes.'

'I can't thank you enough, Jade, and I hope your home is all right. When this is all over . . .'

She walked to the door and pulled it open. She looked out into the alley. There was no sign of the Garda or anyone else. She stepped out to leave but felt Mr Hall's hand on her arm.

'Wait . . . can you just tell me again what my son said? Word for word, so that I can remember to tell my daughter.'

'He told me to tell you both that he is alive and all right and that he thinks about you every day.'

The man's eyes glazed over. His lip trembled.

'Thank you,' he said, hoarsely. 'I can remember that.'

THIRTY-ONE

SHE SAT IN A WINDOW SEAT ON THE RED-BUS. IT WAS ONLY half-full and the driver was standing outside. From across the square she could see some female domestics hurrying towards it. She looked towards the Butterfly Palace but it was obscured by the trees. The driver was chivvying the women along and they clambered on to the bus, puffing and smiling as they went.

The driver got on and closed the door and the bus seemed to heat up immediately. Some of the domestics pushed small windows open so Jade did the same. She felt the cooler air on her face and closed her eyes. She was tired. The last couple of days had wrung her dry. She hoped more than anything that they could all pack up and leave North-Hampton and go back to Peter's Town. Then she remembered the sea had come all the way up to the dyke. Peter's Town might still be submerged when they got back. And even if it wasn't, it would have to be rebuilt from scratch.

She opened her eyes just as the engine of the bus started up. Her attention was taken by a figure walking across the square. She held her breath for a moment. It was the Duke, she was sure. He was all in black and overdressed for the time of year. He had on a hide-jacket and what looked like a cowboy hat. She'd seen them in pictures in the schoolroom when she was younger and there'd been stories about past-world cowboys. The man's gait was slow and steady, as if he were walking on a painted line. A number of people scurried up and began to talk to him. He shooed them away though, with his hand, as if he were swatting flies.

'There's the Duke,' a woman from across the aisle said. 'A nasty man.'

Jade felt herself stiffen. Even though she was on the bus, the presence of this man scared her.

'My brother works for him,' the woman continued.

She looked at her timer. It was at least an hour since Mona had gone with Spike. They would be back in North-Hampton by now.

After a few moments she turned to the woman.

'Why does he wear the hat?'

'He always dresses like that. He likes to stand out. My brother says he has a lot of enemies but no one would dare to touch him. Because of *his* brother, the High-Warden.'

'Oh, yes. I heard.'

Jade watched until the man disappeared behind the trees. The bus pulled out then and headed for a road that led out of the square. In moments, the Saints were behind them and the bus was skirting the town. There were no more flowering hedges or pretty squares, no birdcages hanging from windows, no sign of any of the High-Town people – just the dingy walls of the town that headed towards the metal gates. Jade longed to pass through them and leave the Butterfly Palace and the Duke behind.

THIRTY-TWO

AFTER LEAVING THE BUS STATION, JADE TOOK OFF THE domestic's overall. She folded it up and tucked it into her back-sack. She strode through the town in the direction of the camp, keen to see if Mona was safe.

A bell started to ring and she looked up to the sky. It was one of the churches, she thought; she'd heard one once when she came to North-Hampton with her granddaddy. She continued walking but then another started to ring, joining in with the first. Another and another followed. The sound was coming from all directions and she stood still, listening as the bells seemed sing out together, making a joyful sound.

The townspeople looked startled. She caught someone's eye and they smiled, not noticing that she was from the Wetlands. People came out of doorways and looked up to the sky. The bells continued to make a buoyant noise, as if the ringing was floating upwards like hand-balloons.

A warden came through the archway. He was smiling, holding a small bell and shaking it with one hand, its clapper moving frantically. She heard talk from nearby.

'The high tide has passed.'

'The water's receding.'

'The emergency is over . . . Oh, thank goodness . . .'

People started to shake hands, some hugging each other. One woman began to cry, great sobs, and another pulled out a hanky and gave it to her.

Jade took a deep breath. They could leave North-Hampton.

She quickened her steps and went through the arch and out towards the encampment. She could hear shouting and laughing coming from the homers. As she got closer she could see people emerging from their tents, chattering or calling out to others.

She saw Samson, alone, outside the tent. Alarmed, she walked straight over.

'Mona?'

'It's fine. Spike brought her here.'

She relaxed.

'Rosa recognised her straight away. She and Bates have

taken her to the wash-house. They're going to find clothes for her, dress her up, change the way she looks. I thought you wouldn't mind.'

'That's good.'

'Spike said it went well in High-Town.'

'It did.'

'And we're going home soon!'

'Yes! Did you get all the meds you needed?'

He nodded. Then he looked closely at her, as if he wanted to say something but was stopping himself.

'Oh! I went to see your father.'

'Did you?'

She pulled her back-sack open and rummaged through.

'Your sister wasn't there but I told him what you said, word for word, and he was really happy.'

'Was he?'

Samson was beaming.

'He gave me something for you . . .'

She got the envelope out of her bag and handed it to him. He took it and pulled out the piece of paper and unfolded it. She saw his eyes go from one side of the page to the other, smiling, a tiny gasp coming out of his mouth.

'He's sent a note and this picture. Look . . .'

She took the note and read it. The handwriting was rough, as it had been scrawled in moments.

Not an hour goes by when I don't think about you, my son xxxxxx

She thought of Mr Hall, writing those words in an instant. He didn't have to think about it, he just opened his heart on to the page.

Samson pushed a photograph into her hand. It showed a small boy with a smaller girl next to him. The boy was holding a fluffy bear-toy. The girl was trying to grab it.

'My sister was always trying to take my stuff off me,' Samson said, 'and she was mean; she could punch hard.'

Jade smiled at the tiny girl who didn't look as though she would hurt a fly. Samson's face had lit up. There was music coming from one of the camps and fire-crackers went off, making popping noises here and there. It felt like a festival.

THIRTY-THREE

JADE WALKED ACROSS THE ENCAMPMENT TOWARDS THE WASH-house. Wardens were around, mingling among the homers. They were pinning notices to tent poles:

EMERGENCY STATUS LIFTED
FLOOD WATERS RECEDING

ALL HOMERS TO LEAVE
NORTH-HAMPTON IN THE NEXT
FORTY-EIGHT HOURS

BY ORDER OF THE HIGH-WARDENS

The North-Hampton people hadn't wasted any time. They wanted to get rid of the Wetlanders. Some homers were still celebrating, singing and dancing, while others were already preparing to leave, packing crates and bags.

She went off the main path and took a short cut, walking close by tents and campfires. When she was almost there, she edged past a cart that was being made ready for the next day's journey. A familiar face looked up at her and smiled. It was Kris, the girl she'd been friends with in Peter's Town.

'Jade!' she said.

Kris came around the cart and stood a short way away from her.

'Hi,' Jade said.

There was an awkwardness. She hadn't seen Kris for months and she didn't know whether to shake her hand or give her a hug.

'How are you?'

'I'm good but my granddaddy died. You knew he wasn't very well . . .'

Just then, another girl came around the cart. She had her hair in plaits pulled up on top of her head. It made her look very tall, like a grown-up. She slipped her arm through Kris's and whispered something in her ear.

'This is Jade, from my old village,' Kris said.

'Hi Jade. You want to come with us?'

The girl had already started to walk away and was pulling

Kris's arm. Jade shook her head. Kris gave a wave.

'Sorry about your granddaddy,' she called.

Then she was gone. Walking away, Jade thought about the girl with the plaits and wondered if she liked to read books and talk about the stories. She glanced back and saw them playing with a ball and bats. Kris was jumping from side to side, full of energy. Maybe Kris didn't read much herself anymore.

At the wash-house she found her sister in a curtained-off area with Rosa and Bates. She gave Mona a hug. Mona had a towel around her head and when she unwrapped it, Jade saw that her hair had been cut off, as short as a baby's.

'It was matted. We thought it would be better like this,' Rosa said.

Her sister was clean, her skin shining. She had on some trousers that were too big, belted tightly at the waist, and on the top, a loose shirt. They'd found some boots for her. She smelled of soap.

'She looks like a boy.'

'We thought that would be a good thing,' Rosa said.

'She can have this back . . .' Bates said.

He took off his cap and gave it to her.

'This is a good disguise. She looks very young. A young boy with his family,' Rosa said, looking pleased with herself. 'And, later on this evening I will get her a *W* on her arm. Someone I know has a stamp and owes me a favour.'

'Great.'

It was a relief to see Mona transformed. Tomorrow, she would walk out of North-Hampton like everyone else.

'Thanks, so much,' Mona said, patting down the dowdy clothes, trying to brush off marks that were on the shirt.

Jade thought of the dressing-up-box, Mona's long skirts and flimsies, the beads she wore and the way she combed her hair for hours. She felt a stab of sadness, as though she'd lost that sister and found a completely different one.

They were almost back at their tent when a loud voice cut across them.

'You! You children! Stop!'

Jade looked round. It was the warden with the eye-glasses who she'd seen a number of times.

'Not the medic. You can go . . .' the warden said.

'These are my friends. Is there a problem?' Rosa said.

Mona grabbed Jade's hand and held it tightly.

'On your way, medic. I want to talk to these children . . .'

Rosa looked pained but walked away towards the tent. Jade watched her make her way around a group of children who were playing foot-ball. She went inside and then, moments later, Samson emerged and stood behind a post, leaning out, watching them.

'Who is this boy?' the warden said, pointing at Mona.

'He's from another camp. We've been playing hand-cards,' Bates said.

'Have you?'

Her eye slid back to Jade.

'That's interesting, because I could have sworn I'd seen you around the bus garage today. Then I saw you at the memorial this morning and yesterday, I distinctly told you to stay out of the town. You people are here to shelter, not to come into the town and make yourselves at home!'

'Sorry,' Jade said.

'Which village are *you* from?' she said, pointing at Mona.

Mona didn't speak. She seemed to sway a little.

'What's wrong with you? Take your cap off so that I can see your face.'

Jade felt her neck tighten. Any moment now, the warden would ask to see Mona's stamp. She tried to think what she could say, how she could sort this out, but her mind was empty, a blank piece of paper.

A ball whizzed across the camp and hit the warden in the back. There was a thwacking sound and she stumbled forward, her glasses coming off and falling to the ground. Jade plucked them up while the warden righted herself, coughing and spluttering. Samson came running across.

'Sorry, sorry!'

He picked up the ball.

The warden looked angry. She snatched her glasses back and swung round to face Samson.

'How dare you?! How dare you?!'

'It was an accident. I didn't mean it.'

The warden stared at him. Samson hung his head. She seemed lost for words. Then she pushed him backwards.

'Who do you think you are? You saw me standing here and you did it on purpose.'

'I'm really sorry, I didn't. I was trying to kick it towards the goal ...'

She straightened her back so that she was visibly taller than Samson.

'I know you. You were the one who made all the fuss at the gates yesterday.'

'Yeah ...'

'You held the whole queue up. Something about a fire in your village.'

'That was me,' Samson said.

A bad feeling was worming around inside Jade. She pushed Mona towards Bates and gestured for him to take her away.

'I spoke to some of the homers there. No one remembered a fire. You were lying. That's what I think.'

He shook his head. 'I wasn't.'

'When people lie, it's usually for a reason,' the warden said, pulling her book out of her pocket. 'What did you say your name was?'

'I didn't say,' Samson said.

The warden took a step closer to Samson. She stared straight at his face, her eyes taking in every inch of it.

'So, why were you lying?'

Samson shook his head and started to back away.

'Who are you?'

'Nobody . . . Just a Wetlander . . .' he said, stuttering a little on his words.

Mona and Bates had disappeared into the tent.

'Wait a minute,' the warden said.

She reached across and grabbed Samson's wrist. There was something going through her mind and Jade could almost see the cogs turning in her head. Samson tried to shrug her off but she held on to him.

'Leave me!' he said, sharply.

She had a grip on his forearm and he began to shake it to get away from her. The atmosphere turned ugly. People around them were moving away and from across the camp other wardens were looking over.

'Come here . . .' the warden said.

Samson shook his hand but she held on, her fingers tightening. His bag fell off his shoulder on to the ground.

'I remember. Your arms were burned. Let's see them then. Let's see the blisters.'

Samson stopped then, as if he'd given up struggling. The warden used her other hand to unbutton his cuff. She pulled it back. He seemed paralysed. His arm was in view, plain for all to see.

The pale white skin was pocked, up and down, splattered with scars. Jade looked on with sudden misery. She had almost *forgotten* that he was a feral, that he was illegal, that every minute he spent in North-Hampton was dangerous for him.

'I knew it!' the warder cried out, 'I knew there was something about you. You're a feral! Everybody! We have a diseased feral in among us. God help us all!'

Samson wrenched his arm back and ran off.

THIRTY-FOUR

JADE WAS STUCK TO THE SPOT, UNABLE TO MOVE. AROUND HER there were voices shouting, the warden calling out hysterically. Some children had half-heartedly chased after Samson but stopped after a few metres.

She couldn't see him anymore.

She had to do something. She had to *act*.

She scooped up his bag and started to walk as quickly as she could towards the town. When she got closer, she broke into a run. She glanced round and saw a number of wardens following her.

She ran to the arch. Samson was a way ahead. He turned left off the main thoroughfare, into the alleys. Jade stood very still, her heart thumping. The wardens came running up. She held his bag behind her and made herself adopt a helpful expression on her face. When they reached her, she was relieved to see that it wasn't the same woman. She pointed to the right.

'I saw the feral go that way, over towards the Exchange.'

The warden nodded and then called to the others.

'This way . . . This way . . .'

Jade watched as the three wardens ran off. When they were out of sight, she walked swiftly in the opposite direction, towards the alleyways. She remembered Bates's signal to Samson, so she whistled gently as she went along the narrow passages. It was a few moments before she heard a reply. She waited and then whistled back. Then the whistle sounded again and went on for a while. She worked out where it was coming from and in moments she was at the mouth of a tiny alley.

Samson was sitting on a brick wall, partly obscured by some creeping knotweed. Jade walked towards him, pulling the domestic's overall out of her bag.

'Quick, put this on.'

He was trembling as he unbuttoned the shirt. She tried to look away so that he did not think she was staring at his scars. As he put the overall on she could see that his hands were shaking. She gave him his bag and took her granddaddy's old shirt back. All the while she kept glancing behind, making sure that no one was around.

'You did that to save Mona!'

'I was just trying to distract her.'

'I'm so sorry it ended up like this.'

'It was just bad luck. The wrong warden at the wrong time.'

'We'll sort something out. Me and Bates, we'll find a way . . .'

She felt hopeless as she was saying it. In the distance, she could hear people calling out to each other. The wardens who were looking for the *feral*.

'What do I do?' Samson said. 'You know what the penalty is for being found here?'

Jade did know. It was *a most merciful death*.

'If they catch me, I'll say I forced you to help me get into the town. I'll say I bullied you, stole your money, threatened your family,' he said.

The voices were getting louder, coming closer. Once the wardens had searched the other part of town they would come here. It was important to keep Samson safe for now.

'Go to that place I showed you – the Crow's Nest. Wait there and I'll come in the morning.'

'OK, OK . . .'

'I'll whistle up the steps so you know it's me. We'll work out a plan. We'll get you out.'

'Will you?' Samson looked stricken.

She nodded and hurried off out of the alleyway and back into the town.

THIRTY-FIVE

WHEN JADE GOT BACK TO CAMP IT WAS DARK.

Bates was waiting for her. He looked agitated and was rubbing his head where his cap had once been. The wardens had been there earlier, looking for the feral. They had burst into tents without asking and searched people's belongings. They had been rude and flashed their torch-lights into corners and into people's faces. The homers had denied knowing that the boy was a feral. The warden with the eye-glasses had been taken to a clinic in case she had any injuries. They were probably checking her for smallpox as well. There was talk of a dollar reward and it made Jade feel queasy. Rosa dismissed it.

'People liked the boy. You know that he gave away some meds to help other homers? We don't know where he got them from or why. It helped a man with an ulcer and a woman whose baby had a fever.'

'I didn't know.'

'You were busy with other stuff,' Bates said. 'Samson helps people if he can.'

Mona was sitting in the corner next to Old Mary, helping her with some stitching. The collar of her shirt was up, as if she was trying to hide in her own clothes.

Rosa continued talking.

'Your boy used paste and mortar to patch up a broken wrist and helped a woman in the next camp with a burn when she poured scalding water over herself.'

Jade was taken aback. She'd thought that Samson was keeping himself to himself. Then she remembered that his father, Mr Hall, was a medic. Was that where he had learned so much about illness and how to help people?

'I knew that he had had the disease,' Rosa said. 'I saw the scars when he rolled back his cuffs to wash his hands. He was a good boy, and I don't think anyone here will go to the wardens. Keep him hidden though, in case someone else from another camp . . .'

Jade nodded. Rosa walked off.

She looked over at Bates.

'I need to talk to Mona,' she said, 'make sure she's all right.

Afterwards, you and I will work out a plan to get Samson out of North-Hampton tomorrow.'

'You're sure he's safe tonight?'

'Positive.'

She faltered a little. She couldn't be one hundred per cent sure, but if he'd gone to the Crow's Nest as she'd told him to, he should be OK. Neither could she be sure that they would come up with a plan. Bates hovered for a moment, as if he had other things to say but she shushed him off.

'I won't be long,' she said, 'Then we can work it out.'

She held Mona's hand and took her to the slope above the camp. They sat on the grass and looked at the scene below: the lights strung haphazardly from one corner to the other, the oil lamps flickering at the edges and the fires that glowed across the field as groups of people sat down to eat or just rest.

All the while, Mona was looking from side to side like an anxious house-cat.

'Do you remember when we came here with granddaddy and they had donkey races?' Jade said.

Mona nodded. She was still quiet but Jade felt the grip of her hand.

'Granddaddy and me sat and watched them but you went

to see the minstrels. You remember? You came back doing a dance that you'd seen.'

'I loved the minstrels,' Mona said.

'They haven't been in the Wetlands for a long time.'

Mona shrugged.

'Did you see them? When you were travelling?'

Jade felt Mona's arm stiffen.

'I didn't travel. I just got into a mess.'

'That's all right. We don't have to talk about it.'

'I *can't* talk about it.'

Jade remembered what Mrs Hendrix had said while they were getting ready to leave. *She'll be sixteen soon and the Duke will use her in his club. That's if he hasn't already.*

What had happened to Mona at the Butterfly Palace?

Some children went past. One was holding a bear-toy by the paw, dragging it through the grass. Another had a hoop that she was wheeling. A third had a kite in the crook of her arm. They were skipping along, chattering and laughing. She watched as they went down the hill towards the camp.

'I've got this for you,' Jade said.

She opened her back-sack and rummaged through, pulling out the hard book from deep inside. The words on the front were in large curled print: *The Ballerina.* Underneath was a line drawing of a past-world dancer wearing a stiff skirt and ballet pumps.

Mona looked surprised.

'Granddaddy bought this for me, when we came to North-Hampton,' Mona whispered, taking the book and placing it against her chest. 'It was in the window of one of the shops in Monks' Alley. I was looking at it for a long time. I knew it cost too much but he still bought it for me.'

Jade didn't remember this.

'Tell me about him, Jade. As much as you can. About the time after I left and what happened when he got ill. Please . . .'

Jade opened her mouth to speak. She had lots she could say. She wanted to tell her sister how Granddaddy had cried when he read her letter and how he had searched for her and how he had refused to talk about her because she had broken his heart. She wanted to be honest and tell Mona about the pain she had caused.

But her sister was lying against her like a rag doll.

Now wasn't the time.

'Over the last weeks,' Jade said, 'when he was really ill, he started to talk about you a lot. It made him happy. He talked about that dressing-up box he got for you, do you remember it?'

'Yes!'

'He found it at the pontoon-market and he brought it back home on a truck. Then he painted it purple, your favourite colour, and you collected old clothes and we used to dress up and play. You were Cinderella and I was the fairy and then I had to be the prince when we got to the ball.'

Mona was nodding.

'You went around the village for anything old: a sheet, a curtain, a pair of holey trousers. You sewed them up, stuck on some sparkles and we made up plays.'

Mona seemed to say something then and Jade listened hard to hear what it was. But there were no words, just silent sobs.

'Don't be sad. Granddaddy's last words were that I should find you. Now we can start again. We can get out of here and see what's left of our home.'

She felt Mona nodding and from somewhere across the field, there was singing. Jade listened – it was a camp-fire song about going home. She knew it well. From the field she could hear it getting louder, more people joining in.

After a few moments, she realised that Mona was singing it too.

THIRTY-SIX

IN THE CAMP, ROSA WAS WEARING HER RED CROSS AND HER armband. She was getting ready to go and see a homer who was giving birth to a baby. Mona was going with her. There were children who might need to be looked after, Rosa said. She would also make sure that Mona got the *W* stamped on to her arm. Mona was sorting clean clothes into a bag and seemed happy to have something to do.

More signs had gone up in the camp.

EVACUATION BEGINS AT TWELVE HOURS.

BY ORDER OF THE HIGH-WARDENS

Jade felt immediately anxious. Bates grabbed her arm.

'I've been talking to Mary,' he said. 'She has an idea how to help Samson.'

Old Mary was sitting on a stool, working with a knitting-hook and some red wool. Her pigtail was hanging over her shoulder, curling at the very end. They sat cross-legged by her.

'My dears,' Old Mary said. 'My brother had the smallpox. He had a terrible death. There was nothing I could do for him. I made every potion that I knew of. It was winter and I fixed up a tent outside the village where he'd lived for years. I sat by his side until he died. His wife and children were not allowed to come and see him in case they caught the pox.'

Jade didn't know what to say. Old Mary's hands were moving swiftly, knotting stitch after stitch with the wool.

'Then I had to walk the Wetlands for many weeks until the disease had gone. People avoided me. Even though I'd never had the disease, I was tainted. I lived off charity. It was Rosa who forced me to start working again, who helped me get going.'

Jade thought of Rosa giving her the poppy-pills to help her granddaddy. Rosa helped lots of people, and now she was helping Mona.

'I knew the boy had had the pox as soon as I saw him. He had that pale and sickly look about him. Then I saw his neck when he was washing. He's lucky to be alive.'

'He lost his family,' Jade said.

Old Mary nodded.

'I've seen some terrible things in my long life but taking children away from their families must be the worst.'

'We have to get him out of North-Hampton.'

'But we don't know how,' Bates said, his hand rising up to pull at his cap but dropping again because it wasn't there.

'We will get him across the bridge,' Old Mary said, stopping her knitting-hook for a moment to untangle some wool. 'And it's not just me and Rosa. There are others here who care as well. Many people think the treatment of the survivors of the smallpox is truly evil. This boy is a kind person. 'Course we will help, and we have a good notion on how to do it.'

'Really?'

Jade leaned forward while Old Mary spoke. Her knitting-hook snaked in and out of the wool as she explained. She and Rosa must have thought about it a lot because they had worked everything out. Jade and Bates nodded and said, *Yes…yes…yes…*

Afterwards she gathered up her wool and left them.

Jade felt like a huge weight had lifted.

It was decided. All they had to do was to tell Samson.

THIRTY-SEVEN

THE NEXT MORNING, BEFORE MOST PEOPLE WERE AWAKE, THEY left the camp. Rosa had packed a bag for them and, on their way out, they picked up some food and headed into the town. There were some wardens walking about but they didn't seem interested in them.

Jade made sure that no one was watching as they slipped along the alleyways and headed for the hidden stair-well. As soon as they were halfway up, Jade whistled. Seconds later, she saw Samson's face at the top.

'You came,' Samson said, his face full of relief.

'I said I would!'

She handed over the food to Samson.

'Wow!' Bates said, after he'd given Samson a hug. 'What is this place?'

He was looking over the top rail of the platform. Jade joined him. The water had receded. The ground around the dyke was grassland, strewn with plastix and upturned debris. Some old farm-vehicles and boats had come to rest on the slope that led up to the town. It would all be cleared, she supposed, and the landscape would look as though nothing bad had happened. In the near distance she could see wardens and workmen putting the pontoon-crossing back together. It looked damaged in places and there were machines and trucks all around and a lot of activity. They would fix it quickly because it meant they could get rid of the Wetlanders.

Samson was eating ravenously. The domestic's overall was folded up on the platform.

'They looking for me?' he said.

'Yes.'

'So, how do I get out?'

Jade pulled some clothes out of a bag: a pair of dark trousers and a long-sleeved white over-shirt. She showed Samson the medic's red cross and the armband.

'Rosa and Mary sent this uniform. You put it on. You walk around asking people if they feel OK. The wardens look at you and they just see a medic.'

He held up the clothes.

'They did this for me?'

'They like you,' Jade said.

Samson, still chewing, nodded. He began to look less tense.

'You have to cut your hair. The wardens are looking for a boy with long yellow hair.'

Bates was holding up a pocket-knife. Samson finished what he was eating and took it off him.

'You go to the town gates at fourteen hours,' Jade said. 'Rosa and Old Mary will be going across the bridge five minutes or so before you in a truck. Let them go first and then you go on your own. You mustn't associate with anyone in case you get caught. That sounds harsh but it's the way it's got to be. They'll be going on a truck with a couple of sick homers so you'll easily see them.'

Samson had stopped eating and was trying to slice off his hair. He was struggling with it so Jade took the knife. She stood alongside him, held the hair out and began to saw it moving her hand back and forth. The locks dropped on to the platform. When it was finished Samson rubbed at the back of his neck and jaw. Bates took the pocket-knife.

Without a look at his shorn locks, Samson picked up his bag and handed it to Bates.

'The meds are in there. You have it. If I don't get back, you can take it to Little-Venice. Just so they get what they need.'

'We'll get you back there,' Bates said, a little too loudly, his face forcing a smile.

'Maybe. Maybe not. What's happening to Mona?'

'Rosa is going to look after her for a few weeks. She's going to teach her how to be a nurse so that she can have some work after this is all over. They'll head back to Peter's Town, see if the village has survived. If not, they'll go with the villagers and see where they can settle again. Whatever happens, she'll keep Mona with her until I get back.'

'And you two?'

'We will go earlier. As soon as the pontoon-crossing opens, we'll go across it, head for the pylon and wait with the boat. When you're across the bridge, you leave the others and follow us.'

'What if the boat doesn't work? If the engine got damaged?'

'We paddle. It might take a bit longer but we'll get you there.'

'If the boat's not there, if the mooring came loose?'

'Then we walk and find another boat that *will* get us there.'

Samson nodded.

'It might work.'

'It will work. It *has* to work.'

'Then we'll go to Little-Venice.'

'That's if it's still there,' Bates said.

'But the boats were tied together . . .' Jade said.

'It depends how strong the surge was,' Samson said, buttoning the shirt up to the neck and pulling the cuffs down so that they covered his arms. 'We knew something like this might happen so we strengthened the knots, the straps, the joins. We spent a long time making sure that the connections were solid. There are lots of small craft on the edges though. I don't know if they would . . .'

'Take it step by step. Let's get you out of North-Hampton first, then we'll worry about the rest,' Jade said.

Samson held out both of his hands. Bates took one and Jade took the other.

'I hope – more than anything – that I'll see you two later.'

Jade and Bates were silent as they walked back through the town. Bates's forehead was tense and Jade tried not to notice it. In her mind, she was seeing the boats of Little-Venice scattered about the estuary, ropes hanging uselessly in the water where they'd come undone.

THIRTY-EIGHT

THINGS STARTED TO GO WRONG AS SOON AS THEY GOT ON TO the pontoon-crossing. Jade could see, at the far end, there was a row of wardens blocking the exit. They were stopping young people and talking to them. Worst of all, they were making them tip their heads back so that they could look at their necks.

'What are they doing?' Bates said.

'They're looking for the *W* mark.'

She remembered the bad-tempered warden putting the stamp on Samson's neck.

'They really want to catch him,' Bates said.

The Wetlanders moved slowly. They were five or six deep,

and many people had bi-cycles or carts. Some had children who were being carried or held by the hand. She saw an elderly lady in a wheeling-chair and was reminded of Spike and his brother, Jase, whose legs had been wasted, and the chair that her granddaddy had got for them. It tugged at her heart that he had done such a thing. One day, when this was all over, she would tell Bates.

She'd seen Spike that morning with other ryders coming into the camp, helping to pack up homers' possessions on to their bikes, ready for the trip back out to the Wetlands. Spike had waved at her and said he'd see her some time.

They were inching forward along the bridge.

In just over an hour, Samson would be walking across the bridge in the uniform of a medic. Surely they wouldn't stop him? Not with the armband and the medic's cross around his neck.

If they did, it would all be over.

The queue came to a halt and, when she looked up ahead, she could see the wardens drinking from a barrel, laughing and joking amongst themselves.

It was hot. The sun was only a hazy presence but the heat was heavy. Jade's throat felt dry and she wanted to take a drink but she was saving what she had. She had no idea how long they would be out in the Wetlands before they were able to get fresh drinking water.

They were coming up to the last quarter of the bridge.

'Look,' Bates said.

Up ahead, just visible through the crowds, was a medic, a man in a white shirt with the red cross armband on. He was walking alongside an elderly man with crutches. She could only see him from behind but he had short hair and a large back-sack over his shoulder which also had the red cross on it. The medic glanced behind for some reason and she could see that he was young. Her eyes clung to him and the old man as they got closer to the front.

After a few minutes of her and Bates shuffling forward, she looked away, feeling agitated. The river was calm, the water moving at a leisurely pace out towards the sea. Homers who had reached the other side were beginning their long journey back towards their villages.

Seagulls flew low, interested in the movement across the water. Some people swatted at them but they circled away and came back further along.

The medic had reached the wardens. There were gaps in the crowds where many of the older people were being waived through. A warden called the medic over but gestured to the elderly man to move on. The medic stood in front of him and tipped his head back. The warden nodded and the young man walked off.

It was Jade's worst fear. They were checking *all* young people. If they checked Samson, they would see the stamp on his neck. They would arrest him; there would be a terrible punishment. Suddenly weak, she stopped walking for a moment and felt people banging into her from behind. She moved again, forced to carry on, one step after another.

She felt Bates gripping her arm.

'I know,' he hissed as they were coming up to the wardens, 'I know how we can stop Samson getting caught.'

'How?'

They were in front of the wardens. Jade looked up cautiously, in case any of them recognised her as being the girl who had said that Samson was her brother. Her eyes scanned their faces. They all looked pale and fed up. They were making snide remarks to each other about the homers.

But the warden who had stamped her was not there.

'Head back,' one of them barked at her.

She tipped her head back and the warden looked.

'This one needs a good wash,' he said to the man standing next to him.

Bates grabbed her arm and pulled her away, past the line-up and off the bridge. He was walking rapidly and when they got far enough away, he spoke.

'We get the boat. We bring it here. We rescue him half-way across the bridge.'

He continued walking, veering off the path, away from the train of Wetlanders who were heading home. She caught up with him.

'What if it got smashed up by the flood?' she said, echoing Samson's words from earlier.

'We have to hope that it didn't.'

'If it's not working? If water got into the motor?'

'Then we paddle.'

'But . . .'

It seemed to Jade that it was all useless. Samson would have *a most merciful death*. It would all happen and she had no power to stop it. She was just a twelve-year-old girl. Hadn't she done enough in the last couple of days?

Bates stopped and turned to face her. His voice was loud.

'You can pull yourself together because we will do this! We will get the boat and we will rescue him before he gets anywhere near the wardens!'

She nodded, holding all her feelings deep down in her chest. They walked, in silence, on the track by the river. They continued for what seemed like a long time, getting further and further away from the pontoon-bridge. They passed a lot of debris: old hulks of boats that had been tossed around and ended up along the bank. There was timber and rubble and plastix everywhere.

Soon, she could see the pylon. It stood tall, untouched by the flood.

Bates broke into a run and she followed at a distance. The pylon was looming up in front of them and she could see, bobbing out on the water, the little red boat.

Bates was on the bank of the river. He clambered on to the bush that sat at the foot of the structure. The branches bent and sprang back as he moved across them.

'I'll climb up,' he called.

'Are you sure?' she shouted.

He was thin and he wasn't fit. She was worried whether his hands had enough grip. He was gone though, creeping up the steel frame, one hand on the metal, the other on the rope that was draped down and attached to the boat. As she got closer, she watched him get higher and higher. She picked up the bags and looked around, making sure that there was no one else nearby, no wardens who had secretly followed them.

Bates was up at the point where the rope had been tied. He had both legs around the struts while he used two hands to untie the knot that Samson had made. He struggled for a few moments and then shouted.

'Done it!'

He turned around with his hand holding out the end of the rope. He looked triumphant and began to climb down the pylon and then waded into the river. Jade followed him, keeping the bags out of the water, struggling into the boat. Bates fiddled about around the rudder and found the metal handle that started the engine. He slotted it in.

'Keep your fingers crossed that this starts.'

He turned the handle and the engine rumbled.

He smiled and, pushing away her worries and fears, she smiled back.

They moved off up the river.

THIRTY-NINE

AS THEY TRAVELLED BACK TOWARDS THE PONTOON-CROSSING, Jade watched the homers marching off in the opposite direction. She thought of Peter's Town; the water-tower, the Worship-Hall and the rickety homes built from all sorts of brick and scavenged wood and metal. She felt a longing to be there, away from this place, back to the way it used to be years before. Her, Mona and her granddaddy living on the bay, fishing, scavenging, diving in and out of the water.

But that life had gone.

On each of the banks was the debris left by the flood: old vehicles upside down, the hulls of disused boats, bits of building materials, a section of a roof. Along the way was the usual plastix caught on vegetation or bushes. In the middle of the estuary, she could see plastix shapes gathered together, bobbing up and down. It made her think of Little-Venice again. Had the boats survived the rising water?

After a while they could see the shape of the pontoon-crossing and the line of people moving across it, back into the Wetlands. Jade pulled out her timer and saw that it was almost fourteen hours. Any time now, the truck would come along with Rosa, Old Mary and Mona in it. Samson would follow on. He wouldn't know, at first, about the wardens at the other end. But as he got further across he would begin to realise that he was trapped.

They came up to the shell of an old fishing boat turned half on its side. Bates steered in behind it. When they were comfortably alongside the metal hull, he cut the engine. Jade held on to the rusted rudder to steady their boat. They had a good view of the North-Hampton side of the bridge. Jade could see a truck driving on to it.

'There,' she said. 'Look.'

Old Mary was standing in the back amid a dozen or so other people. She had one arm resting on Rosa's shoulder. Mona was there beside her, wearing Bates's cap. The truck bumped slowly across the bridge. Jade's eyes concentrated on the people walking behind the bus. After a few moments, she saw Samson. The white shirt and red cross were visible.

He wasn't talking to anyone.

Jade leaned forward so that she could see the other end of the crossing. The wardens were still there, in force, checking the young as they went through.

'Why do they care so much about one feral?' Jade said.

'It shows how strong they are. The High-Wardens need to prove to all these people that they're in charge. That's why they'll make an example of him,' Bates said. 'When people witness an execution it makes them more afraid, more willing to do what they are told.'

Jade felt herself shiver. The word *execution* was nasty and she tried to push it out of her mind.

Samson was moving towards the centre of the bridge.

'What now?'

Bates started the engine again.

'We go out to the middle of the estuary, quickly, before any of the wardens have time to work out what we're doing. You shout over to Samson. He needs to get off the bridge and swim towards us.'

Jade looked fearfully at Bates. It was a risky plan.

'Ready?' Bates said.

The engine let out a buzz and the boat moved out from its hiding place.

Bates steered it in a half-circle, seemingly moving away from the crossing, but just as they levelled with the mid-way point, he turned back so that they were heading for the bridge. Jade stood up.

'Samson! Samson!' she shouted.

Some people on the bridge looked round.

'Samson! Samson!'

Her voice was as loud as she could make it. Over on the North-Hampton side, she saw the wardens there looking puzzled, frowning, pointing out towards them.

Samson turned in their direction. He stood at the side of the bridge as people moved round him. She continued to shout out his name. Bates took the boat into a circle and then he let it rest in one place, bobbing about on the water.

Samson looked towards the Wetlands' end of the bridge. Jade hoped he could see the wardens checking the necks of young people so he could understand why they were there, in the boat, waiting for him.

She saw him look back towards the North-Hampton side. Some wardens were moving on to the bridge, edging round trucks, pushing people out of their way. Jade was close enough now to see faces and expressions. One of them was the warden who had stamped her arm. He was pointing to the middle of the bridge and moving towards it.

Jade hollered out.

'Jump!'

Samson looked as if he was cornered. The wardens from the Wetlands side were coming on to the bridge, working their way through the crowd. All movement had stopped, the homers were standing in one place, shifting here and there as the wardens pushed through.

Samson scrambled up on to the rail. He looked both ways. The bridge was unsteady, floating on the water, and Samson was trying to balance. He could have just dropped over the side and into the water. Why hadn't he?

Jade held her breath. What was he doing?

He was standing up as straight and tall as he could. Slowly and seemingly in no hurry, he raised both arms so that his hands were pointing up to the sky. Then, seconds before the wardens reached him, he dived through the air in a graceful arc and sliced into the water.

The river closed over him.

Jade stared at the spot. Ripples were spreading outwards. He was underneath, in among the mosses. She held her breath, waiting for him to come to the surface. People on the pontoon-crossing were shouting. The wardens looked unhappy.

He didn't surface though.

He had on heavy clothes that might have dragged him down to the river bed.

Where was he?

FORTY

'**TURN THE BOAT, TURN THE BOAT,**' JADE SAID, '**I CAN'T SEE HIM YET!**'

Bates steered the boat away from the bridge.

'Where is he?' she said, frantically looking around.

The river moved gently, its wavelets catching the light. Bates was edging the rudder here and there, zig-zagging the boat so it was moving yet staying in the same place. A seagull circled, looking for food, sweeping away towards the bank. Jade's throat was sharp with worry.

Then the river opened up just in front of them and Samson surfaced. He emerged from the water like a fish, his mouth open. His clothes were billowing out and he was taking breath after breath, using his arms to keep afloat.

Jade saw him looking towards the bridge, at the crowds there.

'Quick, quick,' she said.

Bates steered the boat towards him. Behind them there were cries and shouts coming from the wardens. Many of the homers were cheering. Jade reached out and grabbed Samson's hand.

The boat tipped to the side as she dragged him in, river water spilling on to the wooden deck. Samson rolled until the boat righted itself. Water was coming out of his clothes and the red cross had become entangled round his neck. Jade knelt down and worked it free.

The engine throttled and the boat chugged away.

Jade looked back. She saw the truck coming off the bridge on to the Wetlands. Rosa, Old Mary and her sister, Mona, were standing up watching them. They were safe. Her sister's hand raised in a tiny wave.

Samson was pulling off the wet shirt and the armband. Jade grabbed her bag and took out her granddaddy's shirt.

'You might as well wear this. In fact, you might as well *keep* it.'

Samson nodded. He hadn't spoken yet. Water was dripping off him and she could see that his arms were trembling.

'Are you all right?' she said.

'I've been better,' he said, using the cuffs of the shirt to dry his face. 'What about your sister? She get across all right?'

'Yes.'

The three of them sat in silence for a moment. It felt awkward. It was over but it wasn't really. They were out of North-Hampton but they still had to see if the village had survived the flood.

They sped through the water, the town and the bridge far behind them. Jade suddenly felt lost, the events of the last days like a black hole that she had climbed out of. Where was she now? Everything had changed.

They passed the pylon where the boat had been tied up. Then the river began to widen into the estuary. There were upturned boats and bits of dwellings floating across the water: a roof, sections of buildings, a window frame, some vehicles turned upside down. Further on, Jade saw a couple of house-boats tied to each other, beached on the bank, the rear boat askew, part of it submerged. There were no people that she could see.

The others were silent. Samson was peering into the distance, his eyes moving here and there. They continued to travel, just water everywhere now, the land behind.

'Do you think the flood has completely receded?' she said.

Samson shook his head. It was what she had feared. Peter's Town would be submerged, along with many other villages. Everything would have to start again, be rebuilt from scratch.

'Thanks, you two, for getting me out,' Samson said.

'No need.'

'No problem.'

Bates and Jade spoke together.

Samson stood up suddenly, the boat rocking. He straightened his head, making his neck longer. He was like a bird looking for prey.

'I think . . .'

Jade wanted to stand up but was afraid that the boat would unbalance. She sat very still, holding her breath.

'I can see . . . I can see *The Navigator*. I can see its funnel. And close by, there are shapes, yes, lots of them. The boats have stayed together. The connections held.'

He sat down, a smile on his face.

'Where to, Skipper?' Bates said.

'Little-Venice, First Officer,' Samson said. 'Quick as you can.'

Jade felt the boat lift slightly as they increased speed and headed for the village.

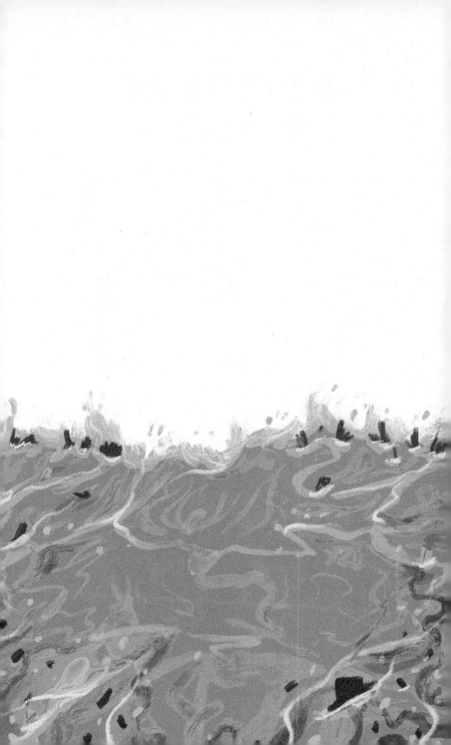

IF YOU LIKED THIS,
YOU'LL LOVE . . .

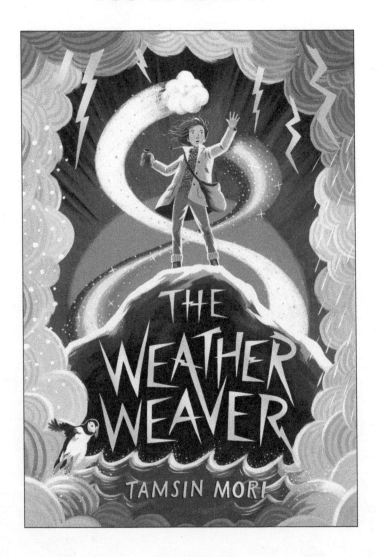

'A MASTERPIECE OF
EMOTIONAL STORYTELLING.'
ANTHONY MCGOWAN

NO
MAN'S
LAND

JOANNA NADIN

Danny Weston

INCHTINN

ISLAND OF SHADOWS

With interior
illustrations by
Miranda Harris

Susan Brownrigg

Gracie
Fairshaw
and the
Mysterious
Guest

Illustrated by Jenny Czerwonka